SIKEVRA

GALESSEL'S TALE VOL. 2
AN ASHELON NOVELLA

Sikevra

Galessel's Tale Vol. 2
An Ashelon Novella

Carolyn Kay

Ashelon Publishing

Cover art, design, and interior illustrations Copyright © 2018 by Chaz Kemp.
Interior design by Carolyn Kay
Editor: Aimee Heckel

ISBN 13: 978-0-9987071-4-3

1. Fantasy 2. Steampunk

First Edition: 2018

Printed in the United States of America

www.worldofashelon.com

To all those who fight for the less fortunate. You are the light in a dark world.

ACKNOWLEDGEMENTS

I have to thank you, the reader, for coming back for book two in Galessel's tale, and to those who nagged me to get this out. I can write for myself, but it's so much better to write for an appreciative audience. Once again, huge thanks to my editor, Aimee, and my writer's group; Fiction Foundry Freaky Fridays. John, Jennifer, Robbie, and Sarah, you all continue to be amazing, and your input was invaluable. Chaz, as always, was instrumental in the production of this book, not only as the artist, but also as my first reader and bottomless fount of ideas when I got stuck. And last, but never least, thank you to my parents, friends, and family for all of your support and encouragement. I couldn't do this without you.

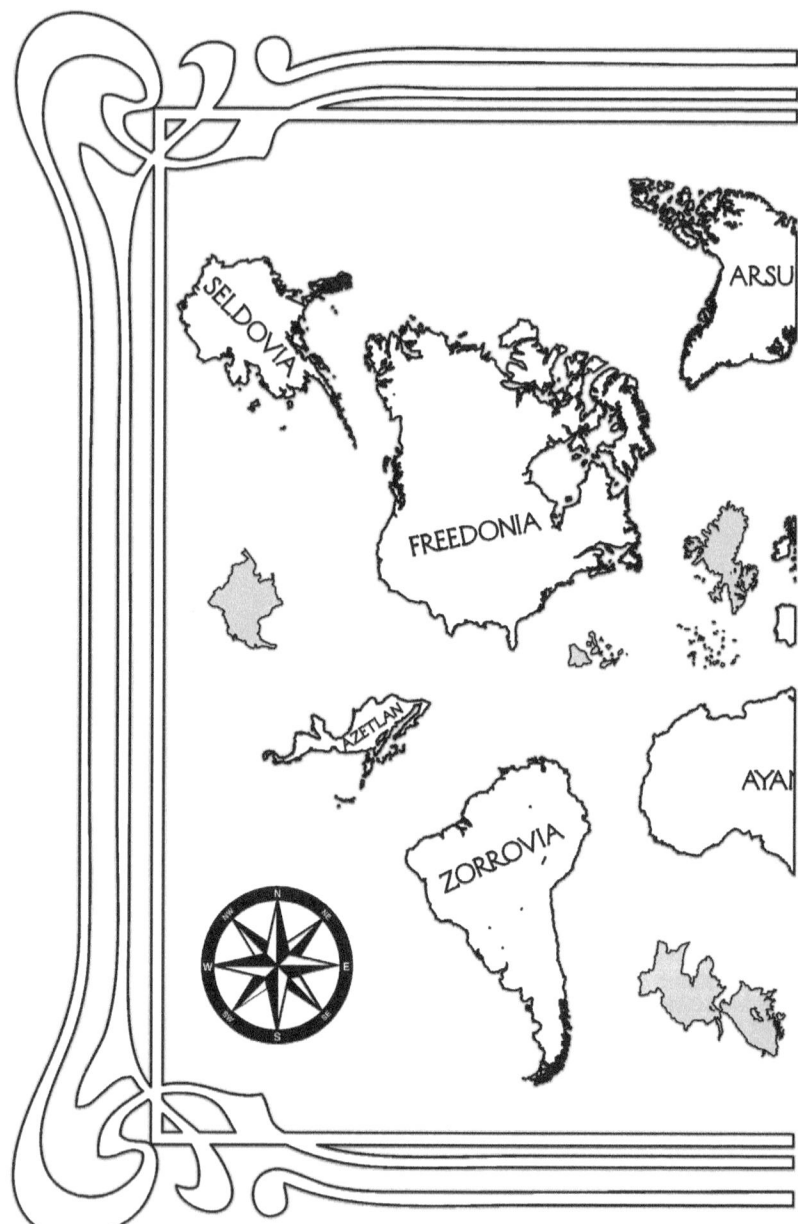

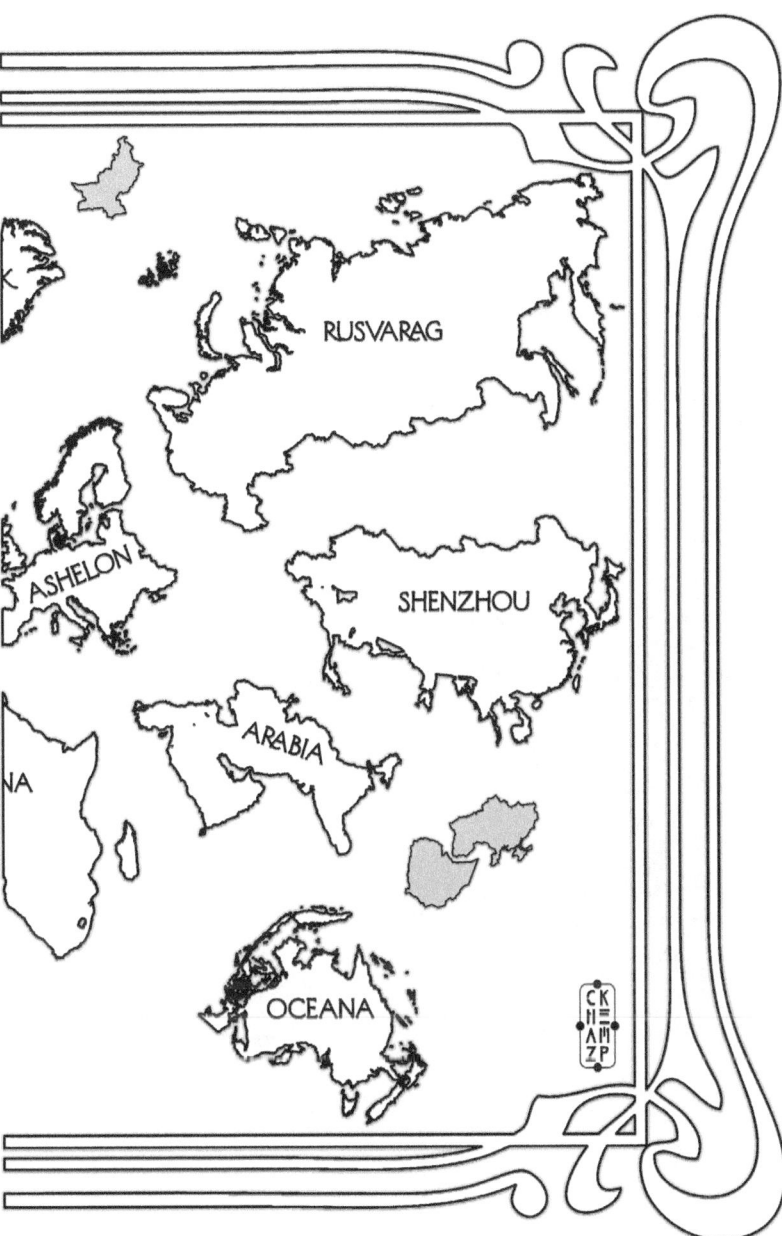

RUSVARAG

ASHELON

SHENZHOU

ARABIA

NA

OCEANA

THE EMPIRE OF
ASHELON
THE YEAR 1850

FOSNA
SVERIGG
LOHJA
SKANE
PRUSSIA
EIRE
SKOTIA
ASHELON
BAVASIA
KIEVKA
GALLIA
SKITAZRA
DEVA
CATALAN
ESPERIA
HELLAS

CHAPTER 1

Princess Galessel cooed at the elfling in her arms. Her newborn niece had a tuft of dark hair on top of her head and lavender eyes, taking after her mother, Miniel. She had her father's dark tawny skin. The child grabbed playfully for Galessel's black braid but thankfully missed. "I will miss you, little one," she whispered.

The brightly decorated nursery was quiet and peaceful. Galessel soaked in the feeling, letting the high notes of the wind chime hanging above the crib soothe her nerves. She was alone with her niece, but the nursemaid was just outside the door, probably flirting with her guards, Erindor and Lanion, who followed her everywhere. Little Talindra was the only one in the castle who didn't avert her eyes when Galessel wore her hair up, exposing her mutilated ear tips. Even though the story of the attack that had rendered them so was common knowledge throughout the palace, people tended to avoid her. An elf without ear tips was *sikevra*— an outcast. At least until the *Fallana Sian* could be performed.

The forgiveness ceremony had been postponed indefinitely because of the actions of the Svellvega, a rogue race of elves who had been terrorizing the fae of the Hidden Lands for hundreds of years. Their vicious attack on the *Intrepid*, the airship bringing Galessel home after a disastrous meeting with Ashelon's Queen Victoria, had left Galessel mutilated. It was an act of war. Her parents had been preparing to move against the Svellvega for several months now, and after a second airship carrying dignitaries to witness the *Fallana Sian* had been destroyed, they deemed it unsafe to hold the ceremony until the Svellvega could be driven back to their ice-locked isle.

But none of that mattered right now. She and her best friend, Clove, had been making plans to return to Arturia, the capital of Ashelon. Their goals: to help the fae there and figure out exactly what was happening to the aid shipments that were going missing. She and Clove's initial attempt to return had been foiled by her ever-present guards, but in the intervening months, she and Clove had come up with a plan to get past them. And to get back to Arturia.

"Hello, Granddaughter."

Startled, Galessel let out a small squeak, causing baby Talindra to giggle. Galessel hadn't heard anyone come in; she'd been so focused on her own thoughts. She turned and gave her grandmother, Analinde, a short bow, holding the elfling close to her chest. "Grandmother, it's good to see you."

Her grandmother tsk'd at her and held out her arms for a hug. Galessel set Talindra back in her white oak crib and obliged happily. The Queen Mother was elderly, but her grey hair was the only sign of her nearly three hundred years. Her amethyst eyes still sparkled with mischief, and work with her own variety of coffee plant kept her fingers deft.

"Planning on going somewhere?" Analinde asked.

So she had been eavesdropping. Galessel couldn't use her silver tongue to convince her grandmother she'd misheard her—her gift didn't work on elves, and besides, she shared the gift with her grandmother. They were both immune to its effects. She had to rely on her wits to get out of this.

"No, just back to my rooms." She tickled the elfling, making Talindra giggle again. "She's just so cute. It's like the light dims a little when she's not in the room."

Analinde smiled, maybe too knowingly. "I used to think that about you, when you were little." She moved up beside Galessel to peer down at her great-granddaughter. "She's going to have the gift, too," she said, her voice soft.

"How do you know?"

"Her eyes. If you look closely, you can see little flecks of silver in them. Just like in yours. Just like in mine."

Galessel stared at her grandmother's eyes. It took her a moment, but she could pick out just a few thin slivers of silver. "Is it the silver that shines when we use our gift? Why has no one mentioned it before?"

Analinde refocused her attention on the elfling, who was cooing and playing with her own toes. "You know how controversial our gift is. It's been used for ill more often than good. If physical signs of its existence were known, those with it would have been exterminated long ago. You and I would not be here." She paused for a moment, letting Talindra grab her finger. "We were lucky for a time. Glamour could hide the silver in our eyes. But that is no more. You must be careful, Galessel. Keep your secrets close. Your silver tongue is known, but the markers in our eyes must never be."

Galessel nodded, sifting through her memories of Lord Davorin. She never got close enough to see his one good eye. It didn't matter. He probably had the gift too. Why else would Queen Victoria ally herself with the Svellvega? But that was a problem for another day. Soon. Galessel kissed her grandmother on the cheek and tickled Talindra's toes one last time. "I love you, Grandmother. I should go."

Her grandmother nodded absentmindedly, her focus on tickling Talindra's belly. "Mind what I said child. And I love you, too."

Galessel was halfway through the door when her grandmother said, "Oh, I have something for you. Come by the greenhouse tomorrow."

"I will," Galessel lied, closing the nursery door behind her.

CHAPTER 2

Galessel carefully folded a green silk shirt, placing it in her pack. She was packing light: only a change of clothes, some jewels common enough to be nearly worthless in the Hidden Lands, but which Clove claimed were incredibly valuable in Arturia, and some traveling cakes. They would purchase or borrow anything else they might need from the family townhouse in Arturia.

She slipped a small dagger into her boot. After the Svellvega attack, she vowed she would never be defenseless again. Clove had been showing her how to use it, and although she knew she needed more time to practice, it helped her feel less afraid. She had also set long, thin daggers into the sides of her corset, and a pocket at the small of her back held a small firearm. Clove had gifted her the corset only a few days ago. It wasn't as restrictive as the ones she wore on her last visit to Ashelon and was actually quite comfortable. She had no doubt the faun would be wearing something similar when they met up.

Galessel tucked the extra bullets for her gun into the pack and tied it closed. She looked around her room. It might be a long time before she came back. There was a time when she would have checked to make sure all of her earrings were hanging properly before leaving her room, but no longer. There wasn't much left of her ears to pierce, and they were still too tender. It wouldn't matter anyway in Arturia. No one there used earrings to denote status. Not like here, where every ring and its placement had its own meaning. Once, strangers would have known her for a princess and ambassador, the third in line for the throne, and more, just by looking at her ears. Now, because of their mutilation, they'd stone her for being *sikevra*.

She ran her hand over her favorite shawl and thought about tucking it in her pack. Sighing, she left it draped over the back of her reading chair, grabbing instead her wool cloak from its peg by the door. She draped the cloak around her shoulders and dialed down the sunstone lamp in her room. To the guards keeping watch just outside her private garden, it would look like she had just turned in after reading late, yet again. She settled down on her bed to wait. She would slip out during the changing of the guard just after midnight.

⚲ ⚲ ⚲

Galessel snuck down the hall, careful to stay in the shadows. Only a few weeks before, her parents had reluctantly agreed to remove the guards from outside her room. No spy had been uncovered within the palace, and the constant presence of men outside her room had been grating on her nerves. Her parents refused to acknowledge the ones who kept watch outside her private garden, or those that followed her from afar when she left her rooms, but they weren't often hard to spot. Those didn't bother her nearly as much and weren't as critical in stopping her escape plans.

She slipped through a servant's door and out into the back garden where she met up with Clove, who was waiting for her by the central fountain. "Good evening, Princess," Clove winked at her, giving her a mocking bow.

Galessel laughed, happy for her friend's antics. Laughter helped take the edge off. She gave Clove a hug. The faun wore brown trousers tied just above her prosthetic ankles and a leather corset much like her own over a light lemon blouse. Galessel felt almost sad at seeing her normally colorful friend dressed so drably, and to know the reason for it.

They waited in the shadows near the fountain until the first patrol of the new watch passed by. After a count of twenty they checked their surroundings before heading toward a giant oak near the west palace wall. Clove bent down, reaching into the hollow under the crook of a large root and pulled out two canvas bags.

As Galessel loaded her pack with the supplies and extra clothes they'd spent a month secreting away, she felt a little giddy. After months of sitting around doing nothing, the excitement for this new endeavor outweighed the fear of getting caught.

"So, you're really going to go through with it?"

Galessel jumped up, her pack clutched to her chest. Her heart fluttered like the wings of a pixie. A glance at Clove showed the faun in a defensive crouch, a crossbow pointed at the former queen of the Anisbarii. Galessel's grandmother must have snuck up on them under the cover of the rumbling airship engines passing overhead. Galessel had to admit that dressed in a dark cloak, with her silver hair tied back, her grandmother blended into the nighttime garden better than they did. She'd probably been following them this whole time.

"Grandmother, I—"

"I've been watching you, Granddaughter." Her grandmother's violet eyes sparkled.

Galessel's heart sank. She'd never be able to leave the palace now. Her mother would have a guard with her no matter where she went. She hunched her shoulders and moved to head back to the garden path. A wrinkled hand on her arm stopped her.

"Now where do you think you're going?" Queen Annalinde led her deeper into the shadows and beckoned Clove to join them. "I know your heart. You always did have a bigger place in it for those with less than did any of your sisters or your mother. It is one of the things that has made you such a potent advocate for the peoples of the Hidden Lands."

Galessel opened her mouth to plead her case, but her grandmother held up a single bejeweled finger, and her words died on her tongue.

"Let me finish, Galessel." She giggled. "You always were the most impertinent of my grandchildren, too." Annalinde paused, meeting Clove's eyes for a moment before nodding and continuing. "Your mother was right to close our borders after the Great Unveiling. But she was wrong to leave our people without strong lifelines back to the Hidden Lands. Would that I had held onto the crown for a hundred years more. But who was I to know the new god of chaos would hurl a giant ball of snow at the world and change things forever?" She sighed, some of the mirth leaving her eyes. "Your parents are doing the best they can, given the circumstances, so don't begrudge them that. Your job, your duty now, will be infinitely harder than theirs, I'm afraid."

Galessel found herself relaxing just a little. Was her grandmother here to send her off? It seemed too good to be true. Her grandmother reached into a pocket of her cloak and withdrew a small, black lily and held it out to her. As it passed through a beam of moonlight, it flashed, and Galessel realized it was made of crystal.

"Take this with you, as a token of my love and protection, and as a reminder of why you do this. All life is precious and worth fighting for."

Galessel's throat tightened and her eyes filled with tears. She took the lily from her grandmother and briefly cradled it in her hands, admiring the perfection of its petals. To turn a flower to crystal was a rare gift among elves. She'd never known her grandmother possessed it. Slipping the flower into her pocket, she hugged her grandmother, unable to speak.

"There now child, don't cry. You will not be gone forever. Those that matter know you are not banished." Annalinde stepped away from Galessel, keeping a finger underneath her chin. "Use your new status to your advantage, Granddaughter. Much can be gained by being on the same level as those you wish to help." She let her finger drop from Galessel's chin and turned to regard Clove once again. "And as for you Clove, I charge you with keeping Galessel safe and teaching her what she'll need to know." She reached once again into her cloak, this time withdrawing a small roll of parchment with her personal seal: a rearing unicorn with a sprig of coffee berries in its teeth. "You're not the only one with secrets, my dear faun. I, too, have connections in Ashelon. Use this if things should get dire."

Clove took the scroll with as much reverence as Galessel had the flower, tucking it carefully in her pack. "Thank you, Your Highness. I promise to aid Galey in any way I can."

Annalinde nodded before walking behind the oak and returning with a pack. "Oh, and you might want this, too."

Galessel shouldered her pack, which was now heavier than she'd planned, thanks to her grandmother's additions. She hugged her grandmother tightly, trying and failing to hold back more tears. "Thank you," she whispered.

"May the Goddess guide and protect you, child." Her grandmother kissed her on the forehead before pulling up her hood and stepping back into the shadows near the hidden palace gate. "Move quickly. I've left horses for you by the pixies' stone circle. They are the best in your father's stables." Annalinde hid a giggle behind her hand. "And I'm sure he will be furious." She shooed them away. "I will delay the guards for as long as I can, but I can't fool them for long."

With one last look at the moonlight sparkling off the peaks of the palace roofs, Galessel took Clove's hand in her own, walked through the gate, and toward her destiny.

CHAPTER 3

Galessel noticed the sudden silence of the forest a moment before her horse's ears swiveled to the right and shied to the left, spooking Clove's mare in the process. Galessel tried to regain control of her gelding, only succeeding in turning him in a circle, when a troupe of fae on horseback burst through the woods. They surrounded Galessel and Clove, their shrill laughter causing the horses to dance and snort.

"Ah, what do we have here? A faun and half-elf out riding in the middle of the night? Why ever for?"

Half-elf? Galessel cursed under her breath as she realized her hood was down, and her ears were exposed. This was not good. She recognized the taunter, a muscular green-skinned fairy mounted on a black unicorn, as the youngest and most rambunctious prince of the Unseelie Court. He was known for his cruelty in general, especially to travelers caught alone at night. She cursed herself for not considering the possibility of this situation. If he discovered who she was, there was no telling what he would do.

If they acted the innocent, simple travelers, the Unseelie would toy with them, throwing them through the air and scaring the horses away, or worse, they'd be killed. If they used their status, then the Unseelie would see it as a challenge and either kidnap them for ransom or kill them.

"Cait Sith got your tongue ladies?" The Unseelie began to close in, cackling and laughing.

"Elfling?" Clove's use of her old childhood nickname told Galessel she understood what they faced. "I think you should look at the situation."

"Oh, there's no need to look at anything ladies," the prince said. "I only question why you are out so late, all by yourselves, and on royal horses, no less? What*ever* shall we do with you?" He smiled, showing a mouth full of pointed teeth.

Galessel suppressed a shudder and looked the prince in the eye. She prayed to Chaun, the god of luck, that her gift would work on him. She put her will into her words. "Our business is our own, Prince Rhazien. And as for what you will do with us, you will let us go on our way, and trouble no one on this road for the next fortnight."

There were hisses of disapproval all around her, but Prince Rhazien simply stared at her for a moment before his eyes flashed silver in response to her gift. His face softened. "Ah, I am ever a pushover for a pretty face, though the ears—my dear you will not win over any halflings with those. But seeing as how you asked so nicely, I will indeed let you pass." As he moved his unicorn out of their way, a puzzled look passed over his face, and his cohorts looked at him as if he'd gone crazy.

"My liege, you aren't just going to let them go are you?" asked a small goblin who clung precariously to a mountain pony. "You know who that is, don't you?"

Galessel knew they didn't have much time before her gift wore off. She caught the prince's eye again. "We are no one of consequence. Prince Rhazien is nothing, if not gallant. Of course he will let us go. There is better sport hunting cave bears than assaulting two pretty travelers."

The prince shook his head as if to clear it, and his eyes took longer to flash this time, but her gift held.

"Of course. Let us away, to hunt more challenging prey my friends." He bowed at the waist to Galessel and Clove. "Ladies, my apologies for impeding your travel. Farewell."

Galessel and Clove spurred their horses forward. As they picked up speed, they heard the troll yell, "But that was Princess Galessel! I know it. And she spelled you, My Lord."

Galessel spurred her horse harder, urging it to fly. They'd just rounded a bend when a banshee-like shriek split the night. Their horses ran even harder, and they let them. Galessel clung to her horse's neck as it tore down the forest road. The horses slowed on their own a few miles down the road.

"Well, that went better than expected," Clove quipped as their winded horses plodded along.

"Well? How do you know Rhazien isn't now racing after us?" Galessel's heart was still beating fast. "That wasn't a shriek of laughter we heard back there."

"I'm sure they pursued us for a while, but that host wasn't equipped for a long chase. Rhazien was the only one on a steed that could have caught us. We're safe for now, but we both know he isn't going to overlook the fact that you spelled him with your silver tongue. He'll want revenge. And he now knows you've been subjected to the *Dien-Vek*. He'll use your 'banishment' as a legal reason to hunt you down."

Clove was right. As an exile, he could kill her, and he'd be celebrated for bringing her head back to his parents, and hers would be unable to do anything about it.

"Well, then I guess it's good we're leaving and heading to a city. The Unseelie aren't much for crowded places. They prefer their prey to be much more isolated."

Clove cocked her head to the side, thinking. "I suppose you're right. But let's remember not to take this road when we come back. Come on, we'd better hurry. We've got people to meet and an airship to catch."

CHAPTER 4

"No matter what happens, keep your hood up, Galey. There are those here who haven't heard about what happened."

Galessel nodded and pulled her hood forward before following Clove into the pub. The Rose and Rapier was a well-known gathering place in Rookemare, a prosperous town west of the Anisbarii Elves' land. Galessel had been there a few times before, but always with a retinue of guards and servants. The pub was neutral territory, mostly due to the fact that it catered to any and all who could pay for a pint. She had conducted a few negotiations there in the past.

It felt different being there now, just her and Clove. She felt exposed without her guards at her side. Goddess, she missed their banter. She missed *them.* They'd been with her so long, they had become more like older brothers to her, and she mourned them as such. Galessel's hand strayed to her ear. She pulled it away quickly, annoyed she couldn't break the affectation. Stroking her ear tips and the rings in them used to bring her comfort. But ever since the Svellvega attack on the *Intrepid*, the feel of her mutilated ear tips brought only revulsion and anger. She tucked her hand into a pocket in her cloak and followed Clove to a table by the bar.

The pub was just as she remembered. Dark woods accented with burgundy tapestries framed large windows that let in the light. A large fireplace in the corner always had a fire and usually a couple of fire daemons sitting nearby, and today was no exception. She nodded to them when she caught their glance, then looked away quickly, remembering she wasn't here as a princess or ambassador. Remembering to keep her identity hidden was difficult. An achy throb through her ear served as a rebuke. Who would recognize her now? With no retinue, no guards or fancy clothes, and absolutely no rank visible in her ears, she was a nobody. Clove was more recognizable as a member of the royal court now, with her curling horns and prosthetic feet.

Clove pulled back her hood as the barmaid approached, but Galessel kept hers up. Even if she was recognized, if anyone saw her ears, they'd call her outcast and throw her out. If she was lucky.

"Clove! It's good to see you. You haven't been around in ages." The barmaid tilted her head at Galessel. "Who's your friend?"

"Good to see you too, Angie. This is, uh, Caley, an old friend visiting from the Lake Country."

Angie turned to Galessel, her face beaming. "Well, welcome, Caley. Don't let the rough exterior fool ya. The Rose and Rapier is the best pub in Rookemare. We've been known to host an occasional royal, as well." She winked and turned back to Clove. "So what can I get ya? Corion's got a fine batch of shepherd's pies in the oven tonight."

As Clove discussed their order, Galessel studied Angie. She suspected the maid was part elf. Her ears had just a slight upturn at the tips, and her eyes were a shade of pale green not normally seen in humans. Not to mention, humans were rare here. The clientele looked to be mostly fae, but she spied a druid in homespun robes in a far corner. Most folk kept to themselves, except for several lowland trolls who joined the table of dwarves. Smaller than their mountain cousins, lowland trolls had been one of the first fae races to live among humans. They loved grueling manual labor and had formed a large part of the workforce that built many of humanity's largest monuments.

"Galey."

Clove's voice brought her attention back. She pulled her hood more forward, trying to sink back into its shadows. She'd been staring at the table of dwarves and trolls too long, and they'd noticed. Now they were staring back.

"I'm sorry. What were you saying?"

"I was saying, keep an eye out for a R'vikki. She's the first mate on an airship that's been shipping a lot of the supplies to Ashelon." Clove looked around the pub herself and sighed. "But we might have missed her. I don't think we made up much time after that little run-in with the Unseelie."

The R'vikki were a cat-like people, prone to distraction and frequent naps. They'd be lucky if she showed up at all.

"How does a R'vikki become first mate on an airship?"

"Marraa," Clove said the name with a roll of the r's, "is apparently quite good with the ropes and sails." She giggled. "The captain's long since broken her of trying to go after the ravela when they show up. Though, maybe that had more to do with her nearly falling to her death after she tried to pounce on one."

"Oh, dear Goddess, she didn't."

"From the tales, she did." Clove's ears perked up. "Shh. Here she comes. Not a word of this to her. I can still feel the scar on my ear where she swiped me for asking about it."

"You never told me about—"

"Hush!" Clove hissed. She stood and walked around the table. "Marraa, it's good to see you. Please, sit down."

The R'vikki sat, twitching her long tail to the side. Thick muscles rippled under tan- and black-striped fur. She wore a leather vest, rough with wear, and a belt with several pouches and a short sword at her waist. Her amber eyes focused on Galessel. "And who arrre you?" Her nose twitched.

"I'm—I'm Caley. An old friend of Clove's," Galessel stammered, her fake name sticking on her tongue. "It's an honor to meet you." She held out her hand, palm up to be sniffed. She knew the basic protocols, but not much else. The R'vikki were normally a reclusive race and tended to stay out of politics.

Marraa quickly sniffed her hand and nodded, before turning her attention to Clove. "I am assuming we can speak freely in front of this one?" She flicked an ear toward Galessel. When Clove nodded, she continued, "So what do you want to know this time?" No one ever accused the R'vikki of being circumspect.

"The *Aberdeen* carries a lot of the goods and food meant as aide to Arturia. Have you noticed anything odd when you unload the shipments?"

Marraa tilted her head and blinked slowly. "Odd? I do not understand your question. Isn't all of Arrrturia odd? It smells bad, the humans do not bathe, and they always want to try to pet me." Her whole body shivered, and the tip of her tail twitched angrily.

Clove laughed. "Forgive me. I should have phrased my question differently. Have the humans ever had you take the goods somewhere other than the normal warehouses? Or have you noticed new or different humans hanging around when you dock?"

Marraa licked a paw and thought for a moment before responding. "I do not usually pay attention to the humans. My duties keep me on the bridge when we dock. But not long ago, a human male came aboarrrd to talk to the captain. He didn't smell like a dock worker. He smelled like hydronium and lilies. A very odd smell." She shook her head. "He wanted to know if we had additional supplies going elsewhere that they could purrrchase. He promised to make it worth the captain's while." She growled, the sound so low, Galessel almost missed it. "The captain turned down the human several times, before the male left. If he'd had fur, his hackles would have been up."

Their conversation stopped for a moment when Angie arrived with food—shepherd's pie for Galessel and Clove and a raw steak for Marraa.

Galessel took the opportunity to ask another question as Marraa attempted to grasp the knife properly to cut her steak. "Was the human one of the normal magisters? Did he look official?"

Marraa set down the knife and eyed her steak. "Official? He was dressed like the paper-pushers, but he had a shiny pin on his coat. Looked like shield with a hammer on it, if I remember properly." She glanced at the steak, then at her paws, and finally at Clove and Galessel. "Would it offend if I did not use your eating tools? They do not fit my paws."

Galessel smiled, then wondered if the R'vikki could see it within the shadows of her hood. "Please, eat as you will." Clove nodded her assent as well.

"Gratitude." Marraa grabbed her steak in both paws and tore off a hunk, chewing only briefly before swallowing.

In the time it took Galessel to eat two bites of the steaming hot pie, Marraa had devoured her steak. The R'vikki licked her chops with a bright pink tongue, and watched while Galessel and Clove ate their pies in relative silence.

Something the R'vikki said tickled Galessel's brain, but she couldn't chase it down. She was just going to ask Marraa another question when two dwarves walked by the table. With a screech, Marraa sprang from her seat, upending the table, and causing Galessel to fall backward in her chair. The R'vikki faced the dwarves with bared teeth. Her tail lashed about wildly. "You stepped on my tail!"

The dwarves held their axes at the ready, but their faces showed confusion. "Begging pardon, but if we did, it was an accident."

Marraa hissed and her muscles tensed as if to pounce. Galessel scrambled to stand and put herself between the two parties. "Marraa, please, calm yourself. I'm sure these gentle dwarves meant no slight to you." She looked to the dwarves, and saw their faces turn from bewilderment to anger in an instant.

"Outcast! How dare you show your face here, at the Rose and Rapier," the elder looking of the two dwarves said.

It took Galessel a moment to realize they were talking to her, and it was then she realized her vision was no longer hindered by her hood. *Dear Goddess, no, not here, not now.* Her heart began to race and her thoughts tried to keep pace. "Please, kind sirs, this is not what it appears to be."

"Sure looks like an elf with no ear tips to me. Which makes you *sikevra*. Don't know what you did and don't care. But your kind are not welcome here." The elder dwarf spit on the floor and tapped the handle of his axe in his hand.

She was not *sikevra*. A wave of heat washed over Galessel. "How dare you insult me so. I am Gal—"

"Galey." Clove's voice cut through the red haze. "I think we should go. Now."

Galessel looked around the tavern. The other patrons were all staring at her. Some with looks of revulsion, some were fingering weapons. Marraa's face was unreadable.

"Go! I do not know about the company you keep, Clove, but I will guarrrd your exit," Marraa growled as she pulled her sword.

Clove grabbed Galessel's hand and pulled her toward the bar and what was presumably a back exit. Galessel stumbled along behind Clove, her mind trying to wrap itself around what just happened. After a few moments, her feet were moving under her own power as the gravity of the situation finally took hold. By the time they reached the backdoor, she was ahead of Clove.

Galessel rounded the corner of the small stable behind the pub and stopped. She tried in vain to slow her breathing as Clove bounded past her, then doubled back.

"Galey, we can't stop now. Those dwarves were drunk and looking for a fight. Marraa will only delay them while it's fun for her, and she gets bored quickly." Clove grabbed her hand, turning to a small lane behind the pub.

Galessel held her ground. "Where can we go, Clove? Rumors of a *sikevra* with a faun will spread like wildfire now. The pub wasn't exactly deserted."

"The plan to hop an airship to Arturia still stands, though it might be a little rougher if Marraa decides not to help." Clove's ears flicked towards the sound of a door crashing open. "Time's up! Come on."

The roar of angry dwarves made Galessel's heart pound. She didn't resist when Clove tugged her forward. They ran.

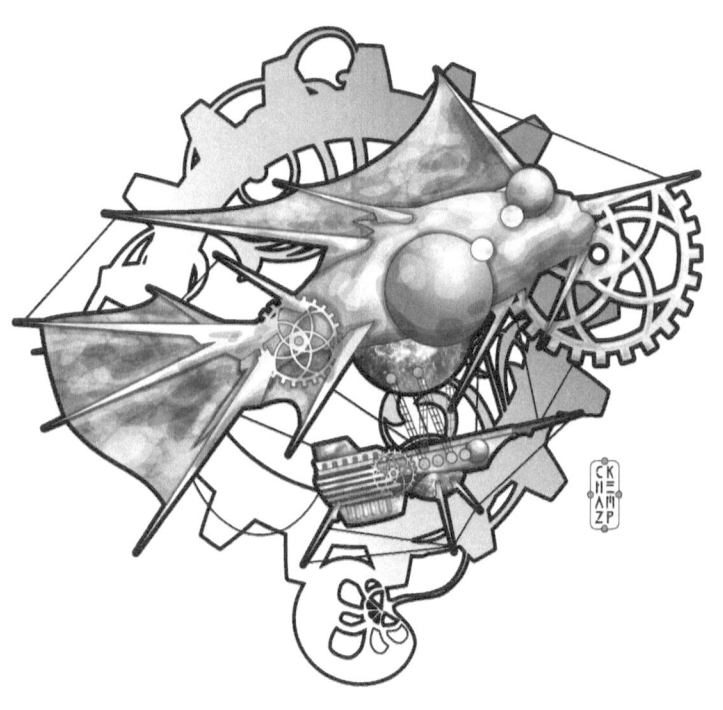

CHAPTER 5

Galessel whispered a prayer of thanks to Donnan, the goddess of fortune, as the sounds of the river docks pierced the air. They'd outrun the drunken dwarves a quarter hour ago and had slowed their pace to a quick walk to avoid undue attention as they moved through the city. Cries of "*Sikevra!*" hadn't followed them from the Rose and Rapier, but that hadn't stopped Galessel from seeing suspicion in the eyes of the passersby. She held her hood forward with one hand the entire way and did her best to avoid eye contact. Galessel felt danger everywhere.

She wondered if this is what Clove felt like the day her family was hunted down and killed. Clove's metal hooves flashed in the lantern light, and Galessel felt a pang of guilt. It was unfair to compare her situation to Clove's. She'd lost only her ear tips. Clove had lost her husband, child, and her feet. Galessel took a deep breath and forced the fear down.

The landing area for the pleasure airships was upstream of the river boat moors, but they didn't take the fork in the road that led to them. Instead, Clove had a plan that required they get there by way of the docks.

A storm was rolling in, dark clouds turning the day into night, but you wouldn't know that here. The docks at the Volaris River were awash in bright light, provided by large sunlamps towering thirty feet above. Both river and air ships docked here at Anisbar's largest port. Fae of all types were here, loading goods, yelling orders from the masts of ships, and doing any of the thousands of tasks needed to ship goods all over the Hidden Lands. The noise was almost deafening.

"This way." Clove grabbed Galessel's cloak and pulled her into an alleyway between two multi-story warehouses. They were forced to slow their pace by the discarded crates and other detritus strewn throughout the narrow path. Galessel was grateful for the respite, and tried to catch her breath as they wove their way through. The buildings leaned in toward each other, making the alley seem even narrower than it was.

The hair on the back of Galessel's neck stood on end, and she looked around, trying to find the source of the adverse feeling. She moved closer to Clove. "Are we near? I think we're being watched."

"I'm sure we are," Clove replied. "Just keep your hood up and keep close. We're almost there."

Clove abruptly veered left around a large crate. Galessel heard her swear and hurried to catch up to Clove, nearly running into her. Clove stood in the doorway of an empty warehouse, her hands on her hips, and her ears back flat against her head. "Chaun is not on our side today," she huffed.

Galessel's stomach dropped. They were supposed to sneak into a crate bound for Arturia. But they'd missed their chance. The crates had already been taken to be loaded. The god of luck was definitely not on their side right now. "Now what?"

"We run for the ship and hope we can find some other way to get onboard."

Clove's hooves rang against the stone walkways, but

no one paid them any heed, if they even heard them over the din of the docks. They pushed past a line of llamas saddled with five-foot tall bales of fiber, narrowly dodging the rancid spit of one, and dashed down another alley to avoid a roadblock caused by an overturned cart of giant geodes. Galessel began to regret wearing the corset. Every time she took a deep breath, her ribs hit the barrier created by the restrictive garment. She resorted to taking shorter breaths, which didn't help, but didn't hurt either.

By the time they'd woven their way through the docks to the airfield, Galessel was becoming faint. They slowed to a more sedate pace as they came within sight of the lone airship at the platform. It loomed above the docks. Its balloon alone was a sight to behold. A monstrous koi fish from the Far East, big enough to swallow a dragon, seemed to swim in place above the blue lacquered ship, held there by gleaming copper chain. The ship, carved with dragons and more koi gleamed under the sun-lamps, casting blue rainbows on the crew that scurried across its decks.

Passengers were queued up at the base of the stairs, in a line that made several zigzags, waiting to board. Two Andreas—pygmy giants—were loading a crate the size of her family's half-horse carriage into the hold of the *Aberdeen*, one of the Hidden Land's largest airships. Their ten-foot tall frames fit easily inside the hold of the ship, making it look momentarily as if it were human sized.

"Come on, now's our chance!" Clove grabbed Galessel's hand and ran toward the hold, only to pull up short several yards away. A dog the size of a horse peeked its head out of the hold and stared at them, a low growl rumbling in its throat. Clove made an abrupt turn and began walking toward the line of passengers.

"Donnan curse it!" she muttered as they walked toward the gangplank.

"Clove, what are we doing?" Galessel panted.

"We missed our chance with the crates. At least for now. The giant's dog would have eaten us and brought its owner a bone as a gift if we'd gotten any closer without being acknowledged by one of the Andreas. We're going to have to get on board as passengers and stow away in the hold after liftoff when the Andreas and their dogs are gone."

Galessel's mind spun as they stood at the back of the line of passengers. She could use her royal influence to get on board, but that would leave an easy trail for her parents to follow. Clove could use her messenger status to get on as well, but again, it would leave the same trail. She sighed. There was only one option open to them that would leave their anonymity intact.

Clove walked somewhat behind Galessel in an effort to hide her unique metal hooves. Galessel kept her hood up, hiding her face in its shadow and making sure to keep her back to the sunlamps.

The steward held out a hand as they approached. "I'm sorry, all of our cabins are full. You'll have to wait for the next airship."

Galessel made sure only the steward could see her eyes and put her will behind her words. "I think you're mistaken, ma'am. You must have miscounted. We have tickets for this flight, as you can see." She held out her hand as if she held a pair of tickets. The steward's eyes flashed silver. She looked at Galessel's empty hand. She was quiet for a moment, then regarded her clipboard.

"Ah, I must have miscounted. Please forgive me." The steward inclined her head and motioned up the gangplank. "Welcome aboard the *Aberdeen*. We will be departing shortly. You're welcome to stand along the rails for liftoff or stay in your cabin, but please follow all directions from the captain or the crew."

Nodding in thanks, she and Clove walked up the gangplank, for all appearances, the last of ticketed passengers. They found a spot along the starboard rail away from the other passengers, and near what they hoped was a way down to the hold. There were too many crew members on deck and in the rigging for them to try the door. They'd have to wait until take off.

Galessel's heart raced as she looked over the rail as the Andreas and their dogs left the hold. She hadn't been on any kind of ship since the attack on the *Intrepid*. The ship shuddered as the enormous hold door was pushed shut by the pygmy giants. Galessel blinked rapidly, trying to clear the sudden red haze from her vision. She felt herself start to scream and clamped her hands over her mouth.

Clove pulled her into a tight hug. "Shhh, Galey. It's all right. You're safe. Just breathe."

Was she safe? In her mind, she could hear the echo of cannon fire, smell sulfur, and taste the copper tang of blood. She had closed her eyes when Clove embraced her. She was afraid to open them again. Afraid she'd still see the world bathed in red.

"Galey, look at me, and breathe," Clove admonished.

Galessel opened her eyes slowly. Clove's blond, horned head filled her vision. Her eyes were bright and filled with concern. She wasn't covered in blood. Galessel looked around her. The ship's crew was running around on deck but not in a panic. She looked over the rail. They were still on the ground. She took a deep breath, or as deep as she could in the corset. The smell of sulfur was gone. Gods! How was she going to get through this voyage? Would she be transported into the past every time the ship hit turbulence? "Clove, I'm not sure I can do this."

Clove took her hands in her own, squeezing them lightly. "Galey, I know what you're going through. It took me years to be able to walk through a large meadow without reliving what happened to me. I won't lie and tell you that you can get past this quickly. But you will eventually. Just remember to breathe. And if you can, think of a happy memory from when we were kids until the terror passes."

It was odd hearing her own advice from so long ago, given back to her. It was the same advice she'd given

Clove after her family had been murdered by human hunters, and she'd been left disfigured. The panic started to subside. She smiled at Clove. "Thank you, old friend."

"All hands, prepare to launch." The captain's voice sounded like it was all around them.

Clove and Galessel gripped the rail as the cargo ship lurched from its platform, the whine of hydronium-powered propellers drowning out all other sounds. The huge balloon would keep it aloft, but it needed six massive propellers to get it airborne. Galessel's anxiety rose with the ship, but she quashed it down, doing her best to breathe deeply.

Clove leaned in and yelled into Galessel's ear, "Come on! We can sneak into the hold while everyone's busy with takeoff."

They moved away from the rail toward the door that would lead them down into the hold. Galessel leaned against the wall, watching for crewmembers, while Clove tried the handle. It was locked. Galessel felt a moment of panic until Clove reached into a hidden pocket in her lime green bloomers, pulling out a small leather folio. She unwrapped the leather strap and flipped back a flap, revealing a packet of thin metal tools. She pulled out two and proceeded to pick the door's lock.

"Donnan blast it!" Clove cursed when one of the picks broke. She fished out another pick and went back to work, mumbling about lazy snitches and gnome-made locks. Finally, with a rather loud *snick*, Clove's task was done. She pushed the door open, giving Galessel a gallant bow, and ushering her inside.

Clove quickly closed the door behind them, shuttering them in darkness. As their eyes adjusted, dim light from below showed them a set of steep, metal stairs.

"Come on, Galey. There was a crew woman just turning the corner as I closed the door. She was looking up when she rounded the corner, but who's to say if the closing door caught her eye."

"Goddess, I hope not. We could use a bit of good luck right now."

Clove nodded in agreement as she pulled a pair of rubber hoof covers out of her belt pouch. Galessel grabbed the handrail and started down the stairs. A moment later, she heard the soft clomp of Clove's now silenced hooves on the stairs above her. Clove was nothing if not resourceful, but it pained Galessel to think of what misadventures Clove had had to amass her vast knowledge of all things covert. She knew Clove was more than just a simple messenger—no messenger needed to know how to pick locks—but she wondered just what her friend had been doing all these years.

Galessel stopped at the second landing and looked out over the hold of the ship. The inside of the hold was nearly as tall as a three-story building and almost as wide. It was nearly as long as a city block. The ceiling of the front half of the hold was lower. Passenger rooms sat above it. Large wooden crates and boxes were stacked nearly to the ceiling there. That's where they'd planned to hide out. But first they'd have to make their way through the maze of carriages, penned animals, crates, and odd contraptions that littered the floor of the rest of the hold. Lanterns, likely fueled by non-flammable moon dust, lit the hold with a cool blue light.

"Pretty impressive, isn't it?" Clove whispered, joining her on the landing.

"Very. I've never been on anything this large," Galessel whispered back. Clove's reports claimed the inside of the hold wasn't patrolled until about an hour after liftoff, but it didn't hurt to be careful. "If I hadn't seen a dragon nearly this size in flight as a child, I'd doubt the ability of anything this large being able to actually stay aloft."

Clove smiled. "That was an amazing day. And one I won't ever forget. It does make the stories of flying Atlantean cities just a little less fantastical, too." She winked at Galessel. "Come on, we need to find our crate and hope it's not buried at the bottom of a stack."

They made their way across the hold, doing their best to avoid the animals, for fear of startling them and raising an alarm. They passed mechanical contraptions that looked like giant men, except where the head and chest should be was a complicated set up of levers, wires, and hydraulics meant to be operated by someone of roughly human proportions, as well as other machines destined for factories in Arturia.

"The gnomes and dwarves have been busy," Galessel mused. "I don't recall all this machinery being part of our trade agreement with Victoria."

"It's not. These are all private acquisitions. Deals directly between factory owners in Arturia and the gnome guilds."

Galessel inspected one of the machines. "These are hydronium powered." She looked at Clove. "That explains the hydronium shortage Leatherfoot told us about. Is it possible Victoria is funneling all the hydronium to the factories?"

Clove nodded, but whatever she had been about to say turned into a squeak when the ship hit a pocket of turbulence, lurching to starboard. She grabbed onto Galessel for support, forcing Galessel to grab the machine she had been looking at to keep upright. It strained against the chains holding it to the floor but did not move.

"Come on. Let's find our crate. All this machinery is making me nervous, even if it is all chained down." Clove released her death grip on Galessel's arm and moved farther into the hold.

It didn't take long to find their crate. One of the last loaded before all the machinery, it was stacked on top of another of nearly the same size. Both were labeled as "Perishable. Do Not Drop or Mishandle." A warning obviously ignored as both crates showed splintered corners and dents in the wooden sides.

"So glad the warnings were heeded," Clove quipped as she stacked a couple of smaller crates to make a staircase against the two larger crates.

"Only the shamans of the Andreas are taught to read," Galessel said. "So these warnings are useless until someone tells them to take care. Maybe Chaun was looking out for us earlier. If we'd been in here when the boxes were mishandled, who knows how we'd have fared."

Clove shrugged her shoulders and climbed her makeshift staircase. A large, unlocked padlock hung in the latch. "Well, at least I don't have to pick it," she mumbled. "Hopefully Marraa will be by before someone else notices and can lock us in."

"If no one noticed it wasn't locked when it came in here, maybe they won't notice the lock's missing if they come by?" Galessel doubted they'd be that lucky, but she made a silent prayer to Chaun anyway.

"We can only hope." Clove gave her a look that clearly expressed her doubt. She opened the lid and snorted. "You were right, Galey. It was a good thing we weren't in here. I think the Andreas played a bit of human football with this crate before they stacked it. Everything's a jumble." She leaned into the crate, sniffed loudly, and pulled her head out quickly, her nostrils flared. She looked at Galessel, her face full of disgust. "Ew! There were jars of pickled salamander eggs in there."

"Were?"

"Yeah. Now they're just stinking piles of smashed eggs and glass. Luckily, there are boxes of cabbage and some bags of oats between that and where we're supposed to hunker down." Clove licked her nose in annoyance. "We won't have to bed down on broken glass, but the stink is going to kill me."

Galessel climbed the small crates and peeked her head in, immediately pulling it out. The stench of sulfur and vinegar was unbearable. She couldn't imagine how much stronger that smell was for Clove. She tried not to gag. She hated pickled salamander eggs. This was going to be a long trip.

Chapter 6

The crate was dark, and Galessel found herself getting sleepy in spite of the noxious smell coming from the other side of the cabbages. As she tried to keep her eyes open, something caught her gaze. Light coming in through a knot-hole illuminated a rune painted on the side of the crate. She pulled a sunstone from her belt pouch and held it under the line of runes.

"Clove, look at this. My runic is a little rusty, but aren't these preservation runes?"

Clove moved to look at the runes and Galessel had to duck to avoid her horns. "Sorry, Galey," she said. "Move the stone to your right...there." She ran her fingers over the line of runes. "You're right. These runes are supposed to keep everything fresh. Those cabbages could be in here for months and still be as fresh as the day it was picked."

"That would make these Fizzlespring Ever-fresh crates. But why would they need them? The trip to Arturia is only a day and a half, and as badly as they need the food there, it shouldn't sit around."

Clove put her finger to her lips and her ears swiveled around. "Shh. Someone's coming."

Galessel closed her fist around the sunstone, cutting off its light. A moment later, she heard footsteps and the murmuring speech of a pair of sylph. The diminutive, winged fae were common crew members on airships. Their ability to fly provided them with unique advantages in the air.

"Ugh. Smells like a goblin's den over here."

"I bet you another crate of salamander eggs busted. Those damned giants still haven't learned to read the word 'fragile,' even after six shipments of the disgusting things."

The voices got closer, and the sound of wings coming up to speed made Galessel's heart race. If the crate was opened, they would be found out. There was nothing they could hide under. But she and Clove tried anyway, pulling heavy bags of flour over themselves. It was suffocating, but there weren't any other options.

"Shyla, I think I found the culprit. This crate looks like it's been kicked around and the lock's off it."

The lid of the crate started to lift. Galessel held her breath and prayed they wouldn't be found.

"Don't! Just close the lid and put the lock on. If you open it, the stench will make the entire hold smell."

"Ugh. Right. Don't know what I was thinking." The lid dropped, and the click of a padlock assured that they were sealed in until Marraa came by with rations. She hoped. It was more likely they would be locked in here until the crate was delivered to its final destination.

They waited until the chatter of the two fae had faded into the distance before heaving the flour sacks off themselves.

"Saved by salamander eggs. Who would have thought," Clove mused. In the dim light of the crate her nose glowed white with flour dust.

"Six shipments of salamander eggs? I thought we were sending fruit and vegetables to Ashelon?" The human's farms still weren't able to produce robust crops due to the weather changes after the Great Unveiling.

"The Anisbarii are. But the humans have started trading with the river goblins for pickled eggs. Apparently they're popular with the military because they keep forever and are a good source of protein."

Galessel wrinkled her nose in disgust and made herself sneeze. Clove's nose wasn't the only one covered in flour dust. "I thought humans had better taste."

"You've been to Arturia, Galey. I doubt you could smell pickled salamander eggs over the prevailing stench of the city. And if you can't smell them, they probably taste okay."

"I'll trust you on that one, Clove. I tried them once, while arbitrating a meeting between the goblins and mudwabbles." She shivered. "Once was more than enough."

Clove laughed. "I ate one on a dare. Lost the bet because I couldn't keep it down. Harsh way to learn not to bet against brownies."

It was Galessel's turn to laugh, but it didn't last long. The gravity of their situation soon sobered her thoughts. "So how do we get out of here when we dock? Even if Marraa remembers to check on us, she'll have to lock us in again."

Clove held a prosthetic hoof in the light from the knot-hole. "With these beauties. If my contact did his job, the nails on your side of the crate are shorter than they should be. I'll just kick the side off, and we'll be on our way."

Galessel nodded. Clove had thought of everything. At least it seemed. Galessel moved around in a vain attempt to get more comfortable in the cramped crate and tried to get some sleep. But her mind kept coming up with all the things that could go wrong. She prayed Chaun would be on their side when they landed. They needed all the luck they could get.

CHAPTER 7

Changing air pressure made Galessel's ears pop, and she shook her head to rid it of the cobwebs of sleep. Clove was already awake, her ears twitching at the sounds coming from the hold around them.

"What's going on, Clove? Have we landed?"

Clove shook her head, motioning for silence. As voices faded into the distance, Clove whispered, "We'll land in about half an hour."

Galessel tried to stretch, arching her back over the flour bags, and immediately regretted it when she inhaled a full breath of pickled egg fumes. She pulled away, too quickly, hitting her head on the top of the crate. "Ow. Ugh." She slid back into a sitting position against the flour. "If I never smell another salamander egg, it'll be too soon."

Clove stifled a laugh and picked a large splinter out of Galessel's hair. "A few more hours and we'll be free of this stench."

"Hours?" Galessel wilted against the bags of flour. "Gentle Goddess, I'm not sure I'll survive a few more hours."

Clove nestled in next to her. "We've both survived worse. Best get comfortable. Our smooth ride is about to end."

❂　❂　❂

"Put that crate over by the door, Jake. Looks like the flies will actually get somethin' this time. Incompetent loaders beat this crate all to Freyka's House and back."

The crate lurched and fell to the ground with a resounding crack. Galessel held her breath. Cracks large enough to see through let in flickering lantern light from the warehouse. But whoever Jake was, he didn't bother to look, and the dull clank of metal feet on wood planks retreated.

"Come on. Get yourself out of that damned contraption. My throat is parched and I could use a drink."

Galessel and Clove waited, huddled together and afraid to stretch at all, lest any sound bring the warehouse workers back. After what felt like an eternity and several foot cramps later, they heard the warehouse door slide shut and a lock click into place. They waited a few more minutes to be safe.

"All right, that's it. If I don't get out of here, my legs are going to freeze like this." Clove scooted closer to the cracked side of the crate. Tucking her knees to her chest, she took a deep breath and kicked. Wood exploded outward, and Galessel recoiled from the sound. When the dust settled, they could see through a hole not quite large enough to let them out. Clove kicked again, several times, in quick succession and the sound seemed to echo off the warehouse walls.

"Come on. If there are guards outside, you can bet they heard that." Clove crawled out of the crate, and gave Galessel a hand.

Galessel braced herself against a nearby crate. Her first steps were jerky and she wasn't sure she could really feel her bum or her feet. The warehouse was dark, illuminated only by the moonlight coming in through windows high on the walls. Her night vision wasn't as good as a murk demon's, but it was better than a human's.

There were only a few crates in their corner of the warehouse. Most of the cargo from their ship seemed to be closer to the doors, and ready for distribution. "Clove, what did that worker mean by 'the flies will actually get something?' Are they going to throw away what was in our crate?"

"No, not exactly, Galey." Clove stretched her arms overhead as she looked around the warehouse. "I'll explain later. Come on, I hear voices outside." Clove froze with her arms partially down.

"For someone with such big ears, you don't hear very well, missy." A tall human with precocious mutton chops appeared from behind a stack of crates near Clove. He leveled a hydronium pistol at Clove. Its trigger was primed. "Get the lights, Jenkins. Let's see what we caught."

Light blossomed in the warehouse as overhead

lamps illuminated. Galessel blinked rapidly to try to clear her vision. When it cleared, she found another pistol leveled at her, held by a smaller human in a dark workaday suit and a low profile hat that did nothing to disguise his balding condition. He made up for it with a red beard that flowed nearly to his navel. A pin in the form of a shield embossed with a square-headed hammer was tacked to his left lapel. Just like the one Marraa described.

"Couple a stowaways, looks like, govn'or." Jenkins said. He sucked on something wedged in his cheek, then continued. "Boss'll pay good money for a couple a flies like these. They look strong enough for the labor gangs."

Galessel struggled as rough hands forced hers behind her back and tied them with coarse rope. Her mind struggled too. *Flies.* That word again, uttered with more disgust than the small insect warranted. Galessel's stomach turned sour as the meaning dawned in her mind.

The tall human leaned down nearly nose to nose with Clove, his pistol now under her chin. He sniffed at her and recoiled, then laughed. "Well, at least you had to suffer through a whole trip sniffing pickled egg fumes."

Clove stomped on his foot, hard. Galessel thought she heard bones crack. The tall one reeled back in pain for a moment, then favoring his foot, put his gun back at Clove's head. "Good money or no, you're dead, missy. There are other flies out there to labor for the boss." His finger began to move on the trigger.

"No!" Galessel pulled away from her captor in an effort to catch the tall one's eye. He kept the pistol aimed at Clove but turned to her. Just what she needed. "You will put that gun down, now." Her heart stuttered when nothing happened, then his eyes flashed silver, and the pistol lowered. "You will let us go and forget what happened here. We are just a couple of people who got lost and trapped in the warehouse."

"Right. Untie these two, boys. Nothing to see here," the tall man said in a stilted manner.

Not good, he was fighting it. Time to get out of here. She turned to Jenkins. "Jenkins, tie up your friends here. They got into a drunken brawl and need to sleep it off."

Jenkins eyes flashed and he moved to obey, going after the two men who'd been behind them.

During the ensuing brawl Galessel and Clove slipped away. They dodged around toppled crates and managed to find an unlocked side door. Clove put her back against the door after they slipped through.

"Give me your hands, Galey. I'll chew the ropes off."

Galessel backed up to her friend and soon the ropes were off. Clove turned around, and Galessel untied her and turned to leave.

"Wait, Galey. Help me find the padlock. It won't hold, but it will at least delay them once they snap out of it."

They found the padlock sitting on a nearby barrel. The door shuddered with an impact just as the lock clicked shut. "Sit on that, mortals. How do you like being caught like flies?" Clove taunted. She winked at Galessel as a string of profanity came from behind the door. "Come on. It won't take them long to get out." She bounded down the alley. It was all Galessel could do to keep up.

CHAPTER 8

"Ugh. I am never going to get that smell out of my fur," Clove said, puffing her pale lemon colored shirt and grimacing at the odors wafting from it.

Galessel and Clove had run from the market district, and were currently walking with the crowd milling toward the factory district and away from Galessel's family townhouse. They could get fresh clothes there and recoup, but Clove had insisted against it.

"You could get a bath at the townhouse," Galessel pointed out. She was tired, and the petulance in her voice was obvious even to her.

Clove flicked an ear at her. "You know we can't, Galey. You know by now your parents would have sent word. There are probably guards there now, just waiting for us. It's not worth the risk."

Galessel wilted. As much as she hoped her parents would look elsewhere for her and probably were, they would also alert the staff at the townhouse, just to be safe. They couldn't go there. She'd known from the start that was a possibility, but it didn't stop her from wishing otherwise. Three days away from home, and she already missed the comforts and pleasant smells of the Hidden Lands.

Caught in her own thoughts, Galessel didn't see the workman, until he collided with her. The impact was hard enough it knocked her hood back. Several people around them gasped. Space around them opened up, and people picked up their pace. The looks she saw as people passed, especially from those who were fae, were looks of revulsion and disgust. One woman looked positively green as she hurried away, pushing people out of her way, and she heard the guttural voice of a troll mutter, "*Sikevra.*"

Galessel yanked her hood back up and far forward, hiding her heated face and her mutilated ears. Clove took her hand, squeezing it in support. Without her ear-charms, no one knew who she was. Word of what had happened to her hadn't reached the fae population in Arturia, so all they knew when they saw Galessel was that she bore the marks of a banished elf. There was nothing she could say or do that would convince them otherwise. Galessel stopped walking. Several people crashed into her, a stone in a fast-moving river, and cursed at her when she didn't move. She couldn't move. Shame had frozen her in place. Clove's hand was pulled from hers by the flow of the crowd. Clove fought her way back upstream to her.

"Come on, Galey. You can't just stand there in the middle of the street." Clove pulled her off to the side, into an alley that smelled like the dead swamps of Nevermere and looked nearly as foreboding. Numbness enfolded Galessel. Would it be like this forever? Even with the *Fallana Sian*, those outside the Hidden Lands wouldn't know she'd been "pardoned." How could she help her people, or even help herself if she was outcast?

Clove snapped her fingers in front Galessel's face, making her blink, and pulling her out of her well of self-pity.

"I'm sorry, Clove. I got lost for a moment. Hearing our own kind call me *sikevra* is still a shock. That's all I am to them here. How can I do anything to help if I'm the lowest of the low?"

Clove snorted and her eyes narrowed. "Snap out of it, Galey. You knew this wasn't going to be easy. I told you your privileged position wouldn't exist if we came back. But you insisted. You're the rebel now. You're going to have to get used to being just like everyone else. Forget about being a princess. Figure out how to use your skills to overcome your new disadvantage."

Galessel stared at her for a moment before nodding. She fought against the tears she felt pooling in her eyes. "You're right, dear friend. I'm sorry. This all just so disorienting."

Emotions flowed across Clove's face: concern, anger, and then resolve. The faun's ears fell and she sighed.

"Galey, we're attempting to dig out the root of discrimination and hate against our people. Humans are notoriously vicious when confronted with their own wrongdoing. I can't sugarcoat things for you, you know that. You've got to toughen up, and quick, if we're going to survive this." She put a hand on Galessel's arm. "Come. What we need is a good meal and quiet place to plan our next move. And I know just the place."

CHAPTER 9

A human boy, his face not yet darkened by even the beginnings of a beard, yelled out the headlines of the morning paper on the corner just ahead of them. "Fire elementals on strike! Cost of smelting triples!" His voice cracked on "smelting," and Galessel adjusted her estimation of his age to somewhere around fourteen.

She tugged gently on Clove's sleeve. "Let's grab a paper. I'd like to know what's been going on since I've been gone." Clove slipped the paper boy a few coins for a paper, earning a warm, "Thank you, Miss!" from the boy. She dipped her head in response and tucked the paper under her arm. They'd read it whenever they got to Clove's "safe place." Clove kept assuring her they were close, but if they went down another back alley she was going to scream.

A few more back alleys later, Galessel was proud of herself for holding it together. Screaming in this neighborhood probably wouldn't help their situation. She was pretty sure a bog troll lived in the alley they just walked out of. She wished she could go back to just smelling pickled eggs.

Clove finally led her back out onto the normal thoroughfare. The buildings were tightly packed, modest, but well-kept. Galessel had lost her bearings a hundred turns ago, but it didn't matter. Not counting her most recent visit, it'd been more than fifty years since Galessel had been in the city. It had grown and changed so much that she was hopelessly lost without Clove.

Across the muddy street from them was a small inn. Stone gargoyles stood guard at the foot of a short flight of stairs that led to a wooden door covered in a filigree of green copper, framed by large windows. A sign above the door was painted with a mechanical horse and proclaimed the inn to be the Copper Pony.

Galessel could feel the tingle of magic as they neared the gargoyles. As she suspected, they were not just decorative statues. But she didn't expect them to move. The sun was up, so they were likely sleeping. Clove ran a hand across the top of the head of the one nearest her. It shivered ever so slightly, a smile curving its stone lips. Galessel did the same out of respect and received a similar reaction from the other gargoyle. The creatures were bound to this inn, but it never hurt to give them a gentle pet in thanks for their service. Making sure her hood was pulled well forward, Galessel followed Clove into the Copper Pony.

CHAPTER 10

They'd spent the first half of the day trying to get the stink off of them. The matron of the inn wouldn't rent them a room until they'd gone to the bathhouse run by her sister-in-law's cousin—or was it her cousin's sister-in-law? Either way, while the ladies at the bathhouse were nice enough, they were reluctant to show them to the private baths until Clove gave her coin purse a good shake. Clove grumbled about how expensive the rackets were getting around town, but only after she bolted the room's door shut and was sure the women weren't listening.

Regardless of the price, the private bath was worth it. A large copper claw-foot tub filled most of the room. An oak wood chair and a dressing screen nearly filled the rest of the space. Sunbeams radiated through the steam-fogged the window set high in the wall, reminding Galessel of her family's gardens in the early morning fog. For the extra cost of a small emerald (which Clove later said was highway robbery), they were given enough fairy dust to remove the stench of their travels from their clothes, Galessel's hair, and Clove's fur. The soap in the bathhouse was good, but only fairy dust was strong enough to permanently get rid of the stench of pickled salamander eggs. It didn't occur to her until later to question how the owner of the bathhouse had come to possess fairy dust at all. It was so highly perishable that bathhouses in the Hidden Lands provided very comfortable room and board to any fairy willing to create dust on demand for patrons. She hadn't seen any fairies at the establishment. Clove had shrugged her shoulders when Galessel posed the question to her, suggesting that perhaps today they didn't want to know. Like so many fae in Ashelon, it was likely they were kept more as slaves than treated as equal beings. It made

Galessel question whether the gargoyles at the inn were there willingly or not.

Seated in overstuffed, royal purple chairs in a sunny corner of the of the inn's quiet common room, Galessel and Clove spent the afternoon discussing what to do next. The paper they'd gotten that morning detailed the elemental strike.

Galessel read below the headline they already knew. Speechless, she handed the paper to Clove.

"Oh no. Gentle goddess, no." Clove's ears drooped and her nose quivered. "I'd heard rumors a rogue group of scientists once associated with the Society of the Brass Prometheus were conducting experiments on elementals, but there was never any proof."

"To what end? According to the article, only a transparent shell was left of the poor thing."

"Energy most likely. With the hydronium shortages, people are looking for other ways to power their homes and gadgets. And the SBP is constantly looking for new ways to power their mechanical creations." Clove slid the paper back across the table.

The whole incident still puzzled Galessel. "But that

doesn't make sense. Why drain an elemental when you can employ it for nearly inexhaustible energy?"

"Because if you employ it, you have to pay it. Unfortunately, like hydronium, the materials the elementals want in payment are becoming harder to get. It's becoming too expensive to employ them."

Elementals, specifically fire and lightning ones, craved minerals like quartz and raw iron ore. Galessel knew both were relatively plentiful in other parts of the world, but Ashelon relied on trade to get large enough quantities to pay its elemental workers. What was happening with all the trade goods? She leafed through the *Ashelon Independent*, looking for more news, finding it on page six. "Royal Trade Minister Increases Tariffs on Goods From Hidden Lands."

"That conniving... Ugh!" Galessel closed the paper and threw it on the table. Clove looked at her, one eyebrow raised. "I should have kept my mouth shut with Victoria. The trade minister has increased the tariffs on goods from home. If I'd been able to complete my duties while I was here, I could have talked him out of those tariffs."

"After what we saw this morning, do you think it would have mattered?" Clove took the paper back and read the article in question. Little huffs from the faun told Galessel that Clove wasn't happy with what she was reading either. "The Hidden Lands are being 'unreasonable' during trade negotiations? Your mother hasn't sent anyone to replace you yet. There haven't *been* any negotiations. This is all fog and diversions to hide what they're really doing with the supplies we're sending."

"We've got to get to the bottom of this, Clove." Galessel sighed and wracked her brain for ideas. The image of the kind, old Dame who'd befriended her the day of her visit to Victoria's court blossomed before her eyes. Maybe she could help "I should talk to Dame Blankenship. Miniel said the Dame always seemed to know all of the court intrigue."

"We can't, Galey. Not yet. We don't have enough information to know what questions to ask her."

Galessel felt completely out of her element. She could talk to nobles, negotiate agreements, and tease apart court rumors to find the hidden truths, but here, among the common people, she felt lost. It was unnerving to feel so out of her element. "So what do we do?"

"We go back to the warehouse district. See how many more warehouses are guarded by men with those pins."

"Ah! That's it!" Galessel stood and began pacing in front of an ornately carved coffee table in an effort to keep her hand from her ear. She really needed to break that nervous habit. Stroking her ears would expose them and defeat the purpose of braiding her hair in thick loops to cover them. She chided herself for getting distracted and brought herself back to the problem at hand.

"That symbol. When Marraa described it, it sounded familiar, but I couldn't place it. Now that I've seen it, I know what it is." She sat back down and leaned in close to Clove, whispering. "It's the symbol of the Hammer Guardians."

Clove sat back, her ears pinned back. "They were outlawed after the Second Great Faerie Riot in 1810. I'd heard whispers of them in recent years but never anything more than that. Now we must go back to the docks. If they're operating out in the open, things just got much worse."

CHAPTER 11

Galessel was thankful for her grandmother's addition to her pack. Though she knew they might be doing some clandestine things, she hadn't packed anything appropriate for nighttime sneaking. Her grandmother had. Bless her. Galessel buckled a thick leather belt around a black tunic. Black breeches tucked into her soft doeskin boots. The belt was well worn, so much so that age hadn't stiffened it. It had several small pouches attached and loops she could slide her corset daggers into. What had her grandmother done in her younger years to need something like this? There was so much she didn't know about the former queen. She vowed to sit down with her and find out when she got back home. Home. She'd only been gone for four days, but homesickness was like a quick jab to her heart.

She rebraided her hair into a single plait, then spun it quickly into a bun, securing it with a sturdy wooden hairpin. A thick woolen cap went over it all, including her ears. The wool itched, but the nights in Arturia were cold, and well, she needed to hide her ears. She pushed down thoughts of the morning and the crowd whispering "*sikevra*" as they parted around her like a dead creature in the road.

From her grandmother's gear she took a small sunstone lantern and hooked it to her belt. The sunstone went into a pouch on her belt.

"Ready?" Clove asked.

Galessel turned to her friend and almost didn't recognize her. The normally riotously dressed faun was attired all in black like herself. The stark lack of color made her friend look sinister with her curled horns and rubber-sheathed steel hooves. "Um, I think so. I have a lantern, my knives. Anything else?"

"I wish we had an image recorder. It would make convincing those in power much easier if we had images instead of just our word." Clove did a mental tally, ticking off items on her fingers. "Do you have the nightroot powder?"

Galessel shook her head. She'd forgotten to add it to her pouches. She dug through her pack, her motions becoming more frantic as she got to the bottom and still hadn't found the blue bag of sleeping powder. With a huff, she dumped the contents of her bag on the bed, spreading them out. It wasn't there. "Donnan take us all! I know I packed it."

"What color was the bag it's in?" Clove asked. Galessel thought she heard a hint of amusement in her friend's voice.

"Blue."

Clove pointed to a blue bag sitting on one of the pillows. "Is that it?"

With a huff, Galessel swiped the bag from the pillow. "Yes. I swear, sometimes I'd lose my hands if they weren't attached."

Clove laughed. "Come on. Let's go."

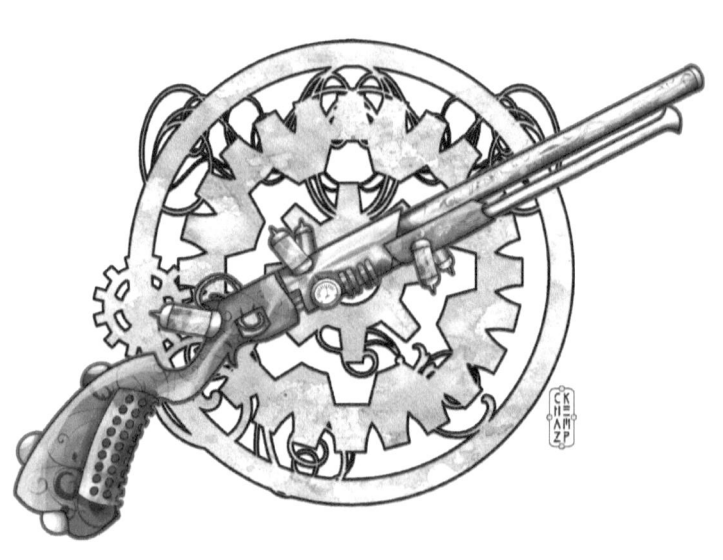

CHAPTER 12

The docks along the River Temese, the waterway that split Arturia, were not as brightly lit as the ones in Rookemare. The humans preferred gas lamps for some unknown reason. But that worked to Galessel and Clove's advantage. They stuck to the shadows, hugging the buildings as they made their way toward the warehouse they had escaped from the day before.

They had already snuck past two City Watch patrols along the docks. As they neared the warehouse district, it became harder and harder to sneak past the patrols.

They were more numerous, and the foot traffic had diminished in tandem with the setting sun.

Galessel rubbed her arms against a shiver as they hid behind a pile of broken crates, waiting for yet another patrol, this time a group of six men, to pass by. The patrols seemed to be more frequent the closer they got to the warehouses. "Are we close?" she whispered.

Clove nodded and pointed across the cobbled street. Several two-story buildings with doors large enough to drive two carriages through stood so close together they almost touched. A sign with the coat of arms of the Queen—a crowned lion and a unicorn on either side of a heraldic circle—hung above the doors on each building. "We need to get around back, and hope the back door isn't guarded."

In Galessel's mind, it took much too long to sneak around to the back of the row of warehouses. She had the patience of a sage in negotiations, but absolutely none for sneaking, apparently. They had gone two blocks back the way they'd come, zigzagged through the animal pens (which reeked so badly she'd nearly lost her dinner), and finally through the alley that would hopefully lead them to the back doors of the warehouses. They didn't encounter more than a few single guards patrolling the back alley. When they got to the warehouse, they discovered why.

They did indeed have back doors, but they were on the second story, and nicely lit by a large lantern. A retractable ladder would allow one to get down, but with the ladder up, it would be impossible for almost anyone to get to the landing.

Clove eyed the distance up to the landing. "I think I can make it."

Galessel looked around, searching for boxes or crates they could stack instead. "Clove, I don't think that's a good idea."

"I don't see any other options. Do you?"

Galessel shook her head. There were two straw bales against the adjacent warehouse, but they wouldn't stack high enough and wouldn't be stable enough for Clove to jump from.

"Keep a lookout. We don't know how often the guards come through here." Clove checked her hoof-covers to make sure they were secure, walked several paces back then with a running start, bent deeply at the knees and sprung up, the pistons in her ankles hissing.

Galessel watched her friend fly through the air. Her breath caught when she realized Clove didn't have the height to make it. Clove's arms flailed as she neared the landing, straining to pull herself through the air. Her palms smacked the edge of the landing. One hand slipped but the other held. Galessel rushed forward, uncertain what to do, wondering if she could even catch her friend if she fell.

Clove was able to grab the landing with her other hand and with some effort, pull herself up onto it. The landing creaked and the metal ladder knocked against the wood with a hollow ring. Clove lay on the landing, panting for a moment. "I told you I could make it," the faun said, laughing weakly.

Galessel took a deep breath, willing her heart to stop racing. "Not funny, Clove." She was about to berate her friend for scaring her when Clove's ears perked up and she frantically motioned for Galessel to hide. There wasn't much to hide behind, so she did her best to melt into the dark shadows between the warehouses.

"Oi! Who's there?" A single city watchman appeared from the shadowed alley.

Galessel kept her breathing shallow, but she swore the guard would be able to hear her thumping heartbeat.

Her fingers fumbled along her belt pouches looking for the nightroot powder. If she could dose the guard before he saw Clove illuminated above, they stood a chance of getting away. She found the bag and with a shaking hand, poured a teaspoon full into her other hand. She had to use her teeth to pull the bag closed again. Slipping the bag back into her pouch, she crept up to the edge of the building and waited.

The guard's night stick appeared first, but Galessel didn't wait for the rest of him. She stepped from the shadows and blew the powder into the guard's face. He sputtered and staggered backward, dropping both his lantern and his nightstick as he tried to wipe the powder from his face. Within moments his eyes rolled up, and he crumpled to the ground.

Galessel nodded to herself and wiped her hand off on her breeches, careful not to let it dust up. The guard would be asleep for several hours. She turned back to Clove. The faun was nowhere to be seen.

"Clove!" Galessel tried to keep her voice low.

The faun poked her head out from the doorway. "Still here." Her nose twitched and she came out to the landing. "Galey, the lantern behind you." Her voice was urgent but calm.

Galessel turned to see the broken lantern had started to smolder against the hay. She kicked it away and scrubbed out the smoking straw. Catching the warehouse on fire was not in their plans. She heard a rattle behind her and turned around. Clove had lowered the ladder.

"Come on. We only have a few minutes."

❁ ❁ ❁

The warehouse was completely dark. There were no windows to let in any light. Clove already had her sunstone lantern out, and Galessel did the same. The two lanterns put off a considerable amount of light, but they illuminated nothing. The warehouse was empty but for a few wooden pallets stacked against a wall.

"I don't understand. Why so many guards out front, if the warehouse is empty?" Galessel asked.

Clove shrugged. She held her lantern to one side, its light showing a walkway that wrapped around the back half of the building and partially along one wall. There was another door. "I bet the warehouses are connected. Let's go see if the other one's just as empty."

There was indeed a walkway between the two

warehouses. The wood creaked beneath their feet but held. Clove picked the padlock on the second door, and they slipped through. There was no need for their lanterns in this warehouse. It was lit, though dimly. The platform was wider in this building, leading to what might be an office. Forms moved on the floor below them.

Clove and Galessel both dropped to their bellies, only inching forward to peer over the edge when no alarm sounded. From their vantage point they could only see part of the warehouse. The floor was littered with large machine parts. Galessel wasn't sure, but they looked like spare parts for the walker/movers used to unload cargo. There were crates along one wall, labeled with "Caution, do not store near alcohol" in large red letters. Hydronium. She counted the crates. There was easily enough here to power a factory for six months or an entire neighborhood for a year.

"And what do we have here?" A large man with dark hair and an earring in one ear loomed over them. He must have been in the office. Muscles strained against his grey workman's shirt as he glared down at the two interlopers.

Galessel panicked, her mind flashing to the assault on the *Intrepid*. She could smell the copper tang of blood, and her ears throbbed. She couldn't tear her eyes away from the man. His visage transformed into the face of the Svellvega who'd assaulted her. She heard the hiss of pistons right before the man crumpled to one side, screaming. Clove had kicked his knee.

"Galey, move!" Clove yelled, pulling at her hand.

Galessel couldn't move. Her legs wouldn't obey her. Her heart beat so fast she thought it might thump right out of her chest. She was panting, but couldn't seem to get any air.

The large man continued to scream. He held his knee in both hands, the pant leg below it was torn and bloody. A sliver of bone poked through one side.

Clove grabbed Galessel under the arms and hauled her to her feet, turning her to face the other direction. "Move!" she yelled into Galessel's face.

Galessel shuddered, the vision of the Svellvega who'd disfigured her dissipated, and her legs finally obeyed her. Clove ran along the landing to the warehouse's other back door. She didn't bother trying the handle, instead lowering her head and plowing right through it.

Wood splinters flew in all directions. Galessel felt a few pepper her skin as she dodged a large one with a sharp tip that was flying toward her head. Following Clove out, she pulled up short, nearly pushing her friend over the edge. Clove's eyes were wide and her ears were pinned against her head. Why hadn't she put the ladder down?

"There's no ladder, Galey."

They could hear men running along the upper landing toward them. "Then we jump."

"But—"

"But what? I know you'll be fine." Galessel looked down. It was far, but not too much so. "You jump. I'll shimmy over the edge and drop."

Only there wasn't time to shimmy over the edge. Two men in black tried to get through the door at once, momentarily stopping them. It was now or never.

"Jump!"

They both jumped. Even with the rubber covers, Clove's hooves rang against the cobblestones of the alley. Galessel hit the ground hard. She tried to absorb some of the shock by bending her knees, but she lost her balance and rolled. Clove helped her up and they ran. Or at least Galessel tried to. Pain shot through her ankle and she cried out as she went sprawling again. Clove bounded back to her and helped her up again.

"Clove, I can't run!" Tears pricked Galessel's eyes as she tried to put weight on her ankle.

Clove looked up at the landing, then back to Galessel. "Get on my—"

There was a hiss from the landing above them, then a splat against a nearby crate. Both women screamed as they were pelted with boiling hot water. They recoiled, looking up to the landing where one of the guards was reloading a strange-looking gun. They ran, Clove helping Galessel, who hopped on her good leg. Another shot hit behind them, scalding Galessel's leg. She fell, gripping her leg, then letting it go, as the soaked, superheated fabric burned her hands. Galessel could hear boots on the cobbles behind them, and she struggled to get up.

"Get on my back, Galey. They're almost on us!"

Galessel didn't hesitate. She knew from their childhood that the faun could carry her without much effort. One quick bounce settled Galessel to Clove's liking, and then they were off. Another shot, this time something solid, ricocheted off the cobbles but missed them. Clove ran, and Galessel could do nothing more than hold on and pray.

Clove bounded down the alleys, her natural abilities augmented by her piston-powered feet. They soon outpaced the human guards, but Clove didn't slow down until they were well within the fae district. Clove finally stopped outside what appeared to be a small apothecary. Galessel slid off her back, wincing as the action pulled her shirt against her back, and again when Clove cried out softly. She tested her injured ankle. It hurt, but she could now put weight on it.

"What was that?" Galessel could feel blisters under her shirt where the water had hit her.

In between pants, Clove said, "Steam pistol. It's meant for riot control—supposed to be nonlethal." She looked at the red blisters on her arm, wincing when she touched one. "But I would hazard to guess if you got hit by enough steam-balls, it'd turn lethal pretty fast."

Galessel turned to the apothecary, noting that the signs were all in Nogoddim, the common tongue of the Hidden Lands. Most fae knew the language instinctively, though it had been reported that some born after the

Great Unveiling had no ability to speak or read the common tongue and had to be taught.

"I know why you brought us here, Clove, but it's the middle of the night. The shopkeeper will not be in."

Clove pulled a ring of keys from a pocket and held it up. The keys tinkled like wind chimes. "Then it's a good thing I have a key." She looked both ways down the deserted street before approaching the door. As she turned the key in the lock, she whispered something Galessel didn't catch. A flash of blue light illuminated the lock briefly before the door swung open on silent hinges.

Clove waved her into the shop, and Galessel followed hesitantly. She felt the tingle of a magical ward at the entrance, but no alarm was raised. It must have been the password that Clove whispered. This had to be more than just an apothecary. Some remedies could be quite expensive, but even so, warded locks and thresholds were not common, even in the Hidden Lands.

"Clove, what is this place?" Galessel couldn't see anything in the darkened shop. She reached for the lantern at her belt but found nothing. She'd dropped it at the warehouse. Clove was of the same mind, however.

A struck match flashed then faded, giving its light to a large lamp behind the counter. Galessel panicked, looking to the windows, afraid they'd be seen, only to see that thick curtains covered the windows. She took a deep breath and faced her friend again. "Clove?"

"I'll explain later. For now, come help me find the burn salve. My arm is killing me."

Every wall of the shop was filled with shelves loaded with jars, tins, boxes, and bags of every shape and size. Bizarre potted plants on a series of tables occupied the space in front of the curtained windows. Several had flowers and buds that turned and strained for the light. The shop smelled earthy, with undertones of spices, flowers, and even rot, depending on where you stood. They eventually found a large pot of salve on a shelf dedicated to ailments caused by or related to heat. According to the label, the salve was good for everything from firewort poisoning and fire drake exposure to mundane burns. As much as both of them wanted to slather on the salve right there and then, they knew they shouldn't stay. Clove filled a container from the apothecary's stock and left several small gems and a baby tooth from a fire drake that was as big as her thumb. It was expensive, but for the amount they'd taken, it was fair payment. She also scribbled a note in the language of the satyrs, leaving it, the gems, and a tooth on a shelf under the counter near the strongbox.

They left as they'd come. Clove locked the door and whispered another word and this time the lock flashed red as it clicked into place.

"Come on. Let's get back to the inn."

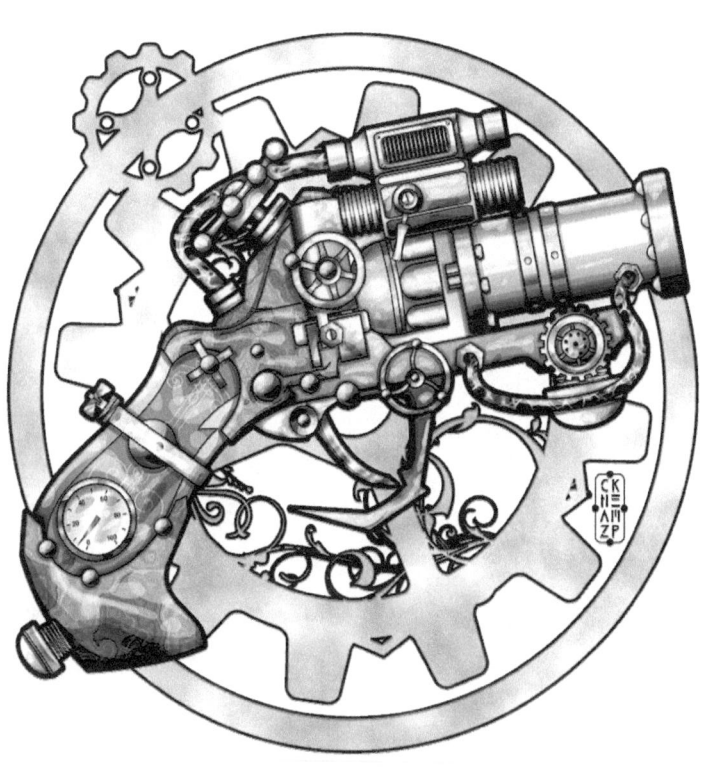

CHAPTER 13

"Galey, wake up!" Clove shook her shoulder. "You need to see this."

"Wha—?" Galessel stretched, belatedly remembering her burned leg. She recoiled, but it didn't hurt, so she stretched again, more gingerly this time. No pain. The salve they'd used last night was truly magical. Galessel opened her eyes to find Clove looming over her. The faun's eyes were wide, and her ears lay back. She held a newspaper in her hand. What had her so scared?

Clove thrust the paper at her. "You aren't going to believe this."

Galessel pushed herself up against the headboard and took the paper from Clove. The headline read, "Warehouses Burn. Fae Arsonists to Blame." There was a picture of what remained of two warehouses—mostly piles of rubble and a couple of partial walls. She looked up at Clove, speechless.

"Go on. Read the article. It gets better," she said sarcastically.

Galessel read it. Her heart sank. She looked at Clove and saw the horror she felt mirrored in her friend's eyes. "Clove, they're not really going to hang innocents for this, are they?" Clove nodded. "But we put out the lantern. We didn't set those fires. And we're not ringleaders of some fairy gang. We've never even had contact with that hobgoblin and sylph."

"It doesn't matter, Galey. We saw something we shouldn't have. And we got away. They're sending us a message."

Galessel threw back the covers and scrambled to get her clothes on. "Come on. We have to go. We have to stop this."

"Galey," Clove's voice cracked. "It's too late."

Galessel froze, her leg half into a pant leg. She

hopped back to the bed and scanned the paper again. The execution was scheduled for noon. "What time is it?"

Tears fell from Clove's big brown eyes. "It's—it's a quarter to twelve. Even if we could fly, we couldn't get there in time, Galey."

Despair threatened to pull her to the floor, but she resisted. "I don't care. We have to try."

❁ ❁ ❁

There was still a crowd at the gallows when they got there. They'd managed to carriage-hop their way to the square that bordered the neighborhood of the fae, but they were too late. The hobgoblin was beginning to turn yellow as its purple blood began to settle in its feet, swelling them like toadstools after a rain. The sylph's wings were grey and flaking away in the wind. It wouldn't be long before she was nothing but a pile of crystallized flakes. The few fae that had been brave enough to attend, if any had, had melted away, leaving only humans in the crowd.

Galessel wanted to run to the gallows and stab the guards with her corset daggers, to use her gift on the hangman and make him hang the two smug-looking humans who were addressing the crowd, but Clove held her back with a hand on her arm like the bite of a bulldog. They kept to the back of the crowd, careful to keep their hoods up.

One of the men began passing around leaflets as the other said, "These two flies, these filthy, stealing denizens of the Hidden Lands were just a few of the rabble troubling our fair city." Boos and jeers erupted from the crowd. "'Fore they hung, they spilled their guts, just like the cowardly flies they are. They fingered these two here, on this wanted poster, as their leaders."

Galessel's mind was still reeling, refusing to see the scene before her, when a flyer was pressed into her hand. She looked down. Close likenesses of her and Clove looked back at her. "Wanted for Arson of Her Majesty's Property—Reward 1000£," the flyer read. In fine print below the pictures was written, "Confirmation of death acceptable to gain reward."

"Her Majesty, Queen Victoria, herself wants you to know that the roundin' up of these two are of the utmost importance. If you see 'em, report them to your nearest constabulary." He bowed, as if he'd just finished a grand speech. The crowd around them clapped and cheered.

"'Bout time someone did something about those foul fairies," a female voice behind Galessel said.

"If it weren't for those no-good, thieving flies, we'd have enough food and the little ones wouldna' go hungry neither," a second woman replied.

It took everything Galessel had not to turn around and set the record straight. Clove's ever tightening grip on her arm signaled that her friend was having similar troubles. Everyone, fae and human alike, were suffering because Victoria wasn't distributing the supplies and food sent by the Hidden Lands, yet the fae were being blamed. She crumpled the "wanted" flyer in her hand and threw it to the ground.

The excitement over, the crowd began to disperse. Clove and Galessel stepped into the shade of a merchant's awning. Humans of all ilk started to file past them: rich, poor, and those in between. While some passersby looked troubled by what they'd witnessed, it was the conversations of a few who seemed to be energized by the hanging that caught Galessel's ear.

"I must say, Archibald, the Hammer Guardians are finally starting to earn their pay," a man in a well-tailored suit and purple cravat noted to his companion.

"Mmm, yes, quite. However, that business with the warehouses troubles me. They didn't have to burn them to the ground to accomplish their aims. We've lost a valuable front for the crown's deceptions." The second gentleman tsked. "We'll have to divert wood needed for the effort to rebuild. 'Tis a shame..." The conversation was cut as the two men boarded a private carriage and were whisked away.

Galessel wanted desperately to follow them to find out who they were, but Clove continued to hold her in place. "We should follow them," she whispered.

Clove shook her head. "No, Galey. We'd be noticed. We have our confirmation that the Hammer Guardians are behind this. I think it's time we visited a friend of yours."

CHAPTER 14

As the door to Dame Blankenship's townhome closed in her face, Galessel took a deep breath. The Dame's doorman, after taking their calling card inside, had returned and told them the Dame was indisposed and would not see them.

"I know she's there, Clove. I heard her." Galessel winced at the desperation in her own voice.

"Come on. Let's take a tour around the park and figure out what to do next. We'll draw attention just standing on her stoop." Clove took her by the elbow and led her down the shallow steps to the street, angling for the nearby walking park.

The Crown had wasted no time getting their wanted posters up around the city. There was one on every other lamp post in this neighborhood alone. Galessel and Clove had done their best to disguise themselves, wearing the one fine outfit they'd each packed—modest walking dresses. Clove's was a pale blue, and Galessel's was green. Clove wore a matching oversized hat, tied with a wide scarf in a contrasting lemon yellow that did a fair job of obscuring her horns. Galessel used a lace and feather fascinator to hide her left ear and used her hair, done in an elaborate, twisted braid, to hide the other. On close inspection they couldn't hide the fact that they were fae, but at least it was harder to match them to the images on the wanted posters.

"Of all the people in Arturia, I was sure the Dame would see us." Galessel wanted to cry but held back her tears. Nothing had gone right since they'd left home. This wasn't how it was supposed to go.

"Galey, look at the posters. I'll bet you a meat pie from the Rose and Rapier that someone on the Dame's staff told her about the poster or gave her one and she recognized you. Even if she wanted to see us, she couldn't and keep her reputation intact."

"So what do we do? Go back after dark?"

Clove laughed. "No, we trick her into seeing us."

"How?"

Clove hailed a passing hackney cab. "Let's get back to the inn and I'll show you."

⊛ ⊛ ⊛

The gargoyles stirred as they mounted the stairs to the door of the inn but did not bar Clove and Galessel from entering. There was still daylight enough that the fact that they moved at all piqued Galessel's curiosity. "Clove, do you think the innkeeper has connected us to the wanted posters?" Galessel whispered. The posters were just as numerous in this district as they were in the Dame's neighborhood.

"I don't know. The gargoyles let us pass, so if they have our description, they either didn't recognize us dressed as we are, or they recognize our true nature and let us pass anyway. This is a safe house for messengers and other emissaries, and they know me. But best be on our guard and mind our conversations in the common areas," she whispered as they entered the common room.

Once in their room, Clove pulled out her pack and dug out a small leather satchel. She traced the rune embossed on the front with a finger while whispering a phrase in faun. Waiting until the satchel quit sparkling, she then unwound the leather strap holding it closed and spread the opened satchel across the bed. It contained several pockets filled with stationery—some plain, some with official letterhead—and several pockets of wax seals on linen, carefully wrapped to avoid breakage.

"Now, who do you think the Dame would most like to take tea with tomorrow?" Clove leafed through the printed letterhead. "Lady Chastworthy of Dunham? Dame Elphonse of Quinthaven? Or possibly Baronessa di Tripoli from Esperia?"

"How on earth did you get stationary from nobility in Esperia?" Galessel knew her friend was well-traveled, but the Hidden Lands didn't have many ties there. Centuries of fanatical religious rule in the country had led to the destruction of most of the Ways between the two realms, and travel there was still perilous for the fae.

Clove winked at her. "Even the most careful nobles lose things during travel. I'm just lucky enough to find them before they do." The faun dug through her pack again and pulled out the rolled parchment Galessel's grandmother had given her. "We can always use this."

Galessel held out her hand and Clove passed her
the parchment. Her grandmother's seal was still intact.
She'd forgotten about this until Clove had unearthed
it. What was inside? There was only one way to know.
She placed her palm over the seal. It felt warm to the
touch, as if it'd been freshly poured and pressed. Magic.
Goddess bless her grandmother. She knew they might
have need to open it without breaking the seal. Galessel
whispered the family password. The seal popped from
the parchment, intact. She laid it carefully on the bed,
then unrolled the missive.

*"By order of the Queen Mother, Annalinde
Avandi, whosoever bears this missive is to be
granted whatever aid they request. All expenses
incurred while rendering such aid will be paid
by the House Avandi, Rulers of the Hidden
Lands, and sovereigns of the Anisbarii Elves."*

It was signed with her grandmother's crisp signature.
Galessel handed the parchment to Clove, who read it
silently. "Well, this could come in handy. But tea at the
Broadbury should lure the Dame away, and we can keep
your grandmother's scroll for later."

Galessel nodded and hoped they'd never have need
of the scroll. She carefully rerolled the parchment and

replaced the seal, speaking the password once again. The seal warmed, adhering to the scroll. She handed it back to Clove to secret away.

Clove pulled a quill, ink bottle, and the stationary from her satchel and took it over to the small desk in the corner of the room. "The Baronessa is the safest choice. She's not likely to show up at the Broadbury for tea on the same day by chance. I'm going to draft an invitation, and you can tell me if it's sufficiently haughty for a noble."

Galessel stuck her tongue out at the back of Clove's head. Clove had dressed her down on more than one occasion for being a "stuck-up royal," but she knew the faun was just poking fun. How she longed for the days when she and Clove spent more time being silly than serious. The image of the dead fae in the square floated before her eyes, and she felt tears begin to pool. She let the tears fall, sobbing quietly so as to not disturb Clove. They were dead because of her. Because she couldn't leave well enough alone. But if she didn't get to the bottom of this, more fae from the Hidden Lands, and human commoners, would starve. *Gentle Goddess, guide those two poor souls to the Fair Lands. Whatever*

marks they had against them, give to me, for they died
because of my actions. Grant me strength to right these
wrongs and see justice done.

Clove turned around, the stationary held before her
like a herald. Galessel quickly wiped away her tears, but
not before Clove saw them.

"Oh, Galey." Clove set the stationary on the desk and
came to sit down on the bed, enfolding Galessel in a hug.
"We'll get those thugs who did this. They won't get away
with it."

Clove's hug brought fresh tears, and Galessel sobbed
into the faun's shoulder. "If we'd gotten there sooner—"

Clove pushed back. "Oh no you don't. If we'd gotten
there sooner, you would have used your gift. And maybe
we could have saved them. Maybe we could have even
gotten away. But word would have gotten back to
Victoria that you were in Arturia, and she'd probably
hang even more of our kin to send you a message." The
faun shook her head. "What's done is done. Mourn for
those two, but stop beating yourself up over what could
have been, and help me get this invitation right so we
can move forward." Clove gave her another hug and
moved back to the desk.

Galessel wasn't sure, but she thought she saw her friend wipe away a tear or two as she turned back to the task at hand.

Clove read:

"Dear Dame Blankenship,

The Baronessa di Tripoli requests your company for high tea on the fifth of April at the Broadbury, Arturia.

Send reply with my messenger.

Regards,

Constintina Romera Maria deMarco,

Baronessa di Tripoli"

"I would say 'requests the *pleasure* of your company.' Otherwise, it sounds reasonable for a noble."

A knock on the door made both women jump. Clove's ears laid back against her head. "Yes?"

"A message for you, Miss" came the muffled reply.

Clove rose and opened the door a crack. She accepted the folded parchment and retrieved a coin from her purse for the maid. "Thank you."

Closing the door behind her, she listened for a moment, before returning to the bed and examining the letter.

"It's from Blankenship," Clove said, surprise in her voice. She handed the letter to Galessel and went back to the door, holding her ear to it. "All right, no one's out there. Open it."

Galessel broke the wax seal and read the letter, written in a very neat hand.

The pleasure of your company is requested at half past ten this evening to survey the renovations to my underground solarium. A carriage will arrive at ten o'clock to convey you. Please wear protective clothing, as the bees tend to be temperamental, even in the late evening.

Sincerely yours,

DB

The old woman was crafty, Galessel had to give her that. But something didn't quite feel right. "Do you think it's a trap? Do you think we were followed today?" She handed the letter to Clove.

Clove shook her head. "By the Hammer Guardians? I don't think so. The message is a little cryptic. If it was a trap, the wording would be more plain. And the handwriting style is definitely from someone who learned to write before the Great Unveiling. It's too rounded for modern script and definitely from a feminine hand."

Galessel had to defer to Clove's experience there. Human writing style was something she had no experience with. "Miniel said she was quite crafty. I wouldn't put it past her to have her own spies. I think we can safely assume then, that she doesn't actually mean we should dress as beekeepers."

"A good thing, too. I don't have any idea where we'd get outfits like that," Clove giggled.

Galessel felt herself relax just a little bit. If the Dame was willing to meet with them, even in secret, maybe it meant things were finally starting to go their way.

WANTED

FOR ARSON OF HER MAJESTY'S PROPERTY

REWARD 1000£

CONFIRMATION OF DEATH ACCEPTABLE TO GAIN REWARD

CHAPTER 15

The carriage driver pulled his horse to a stop in the alley. "This is it. End o' the line, ladies."

To Galessel's eye, it was an alley like any other in Arturia. Except maybe it smelled a little better and was wide enough for a small trap to traverse. The night was cloudy, and what little moonlight there was showed her only some discarded boxes and a few scurrying shadows.

"Are you sure?" Galessel asked.

"Aye. This is where I was told to let you off. If you want to go back to the Copper Pony, it'll cost you two quid. The gent who hired me didn't pay for a return trip."

Galessel looked at Clove, unsure.

Clove shrugged. "We've come this far."

The driver clicked to his horse and was gone before either of them could say thank you, taking the trap's lantern light with it. Clove's nose flared as she sniffed the air. "There's no one else around. We can unshutter the lantern."

Galessel opened the shutter, and the alley around them was revealed. Even in the light, there was still nothing remarkable about where they stood. "So what now, Clove? The Dame mentioned an underground solarium, but I see no doors." There were no windows that looked into the alley either, for that matter. It reminded her a little of the alley in the fae market, which sparked a thought. "Did you read anything in the message that might indicate a secret door?"

Clove thought about it, and shrugged. "No. But give me the lantern. I think I see something."

Galessel handed over the lantern and followed her friend as she walked farther down the alley, stopping in front of a pair of cellar doors painted to look like the surrounding brick walls. Clove knelt and put her ear to the door. "I hear someone grumbling about 'being late.' I'm guessing this is our entrance."

Clove took a look around the alley. Satisfied they were alone, she knocked on the door. It was answered with the sound a bolt sliding free.

One of the doors eased open a crack. A voice from within whispered, "Who's the eldest daughter of the Queen of the Elves?"

"Miniel of Anisbar," Clove replied.

The door opened wider, and Dame Blankenship's butler's head appeared. "Right then, follow me. Quickly. No one knows about these tunnels and we'd like to keep it that way. Hurry now."

Clove and Galessel did as they were bidden, stepping carefully down the short flight of wooden stairs into a masonry tunnel. The butler hadn't waited for them. The light from his lantern retreated into the tunnel.

"Did you know about these tunnels, Clove?" Galessel whispered as they hurried to catch up to the butler.

"No, but now I'm curious how many of these exist."

"You could lose your head for knowing such things, Miss," the butler said, looking over his shoulder at them. Disapproval showed plain in his eyes.

They walked the rest of the way in silence, past bricked-up side tunnels and through enough turns that Galessel wasn't sure she could get back to the alley without a guide. A sudden chill caused her to wrap her scarf tighter around her neck. Both she and Clove wore thick scarves over their heads, interpreting Dame Blankenship's instructions as ones to cover their obviously fae features to avoid suspicion.

At last they came to another wooden stairway and followed the butler up and through a stout oak door. The butler let them pass, then closed the door and bolted it shut with an elaborate clockwork goblin lock. He began to push a stack of empty wooden crates in front of the door. "Up those stairs, down the hall, second door on the right. My mistress is waiting for you."

Clove glanced at Galessel, shrugged, and started down the hall. It was a breach of protocol as far as Galessel knew to not be preceded by the butler and announced, but this was not a normal visit.

They found the Dame seated in her living room, bundled in a thick green robe, her grey hair pulled back in a simple twist, sipping a turquoise liquid from a delicate crystal glass. Galessel could smell cinnamon and toasted almonds. She looked around the elegantly appointed room, her eyes finally finding what they sought. A bottle formed with a hole in the middle, capped with a carved wooden acorn, sat on the sideboard next to two more of the small glasses. How did the Dame come to own a bottle of elven schnapps? It was rare even in the Hidden Lands and not part of any shipments to Arturia.

Dame Blankenship rose to greet them. "Ah good, you got my message." She took Galessel's hands in hers and kissed her once on each cheek. "I'm sorry I had to turn you away earlier. I was expecting another visitor, and the maid had just brought in the mail. She went on a rant on the spot about the fae and how they're ruining Arturia. Needless to say, she's now looking for other employment."

"I do appreciate you seeing us so late, and taking the chance on us, madam. May I present, Clove, my family's personal messenger and my best friend."

Clove curtsied, but the Dame would have none of it and greeted Clove the same way she had Galessel.

"Come, sit." The elderly noble indicated the saffron brocade couch and made her way to the sideboard, bringing back two glasses of schnapps, handing one to each of them before taking a seat in a very plush looking chair. "To rebellious spirits," she toasted.

Galessel and Clove echoed the toast and sipped from their glasses. The liquid burned on the way down, but not in an unpleasant way. The Dame turned to Galessel. "You can remove your scarf, child. I heard about your horrific ordeal after leaving the palace the last we met. Disgraced and then assaulted. I can't imagine." She shook her head. "Were the scoundrels who did that ever caught? Is that why you came back?"

Galessel and Clove both removed their scarves. Dame Blankenship glanced at Galessel's ears before her gaze was caught by the sight of Clove's horns.

"The pirates who did this to me are dead," Galessel said, surprised at the vehemence in her voice. "But the one behind the attack still sits at Victoria's right hand."

The Dame didn't look surprised at the news. Was she allied with Victoria or just a shrewd woman? Logic told Galessel if she'd wanted to turn them in, the elderly noble would have had guards meet them at the tunnel, not her butler. Besides, why waste very expensive liquor on an enemy? She decided to push forward. "Madame, it pains me to put you in danger by coming here, but we need your help."

"Oh, I ferreted out as much when you came by earlier. What have you gotten yourself into, child?"

Between the two of them, Galessel and Clove told the story of the missing shipments of food and supplies and the systemic abuse of the fae in Arturia. The Dame listened intently, visibly troubled when they told her of the lynching of the two innocents earlier.

"And you suspect Victoria of being behind this?" the Dame asked when they'd finished.

"If not her, then others with enough power to pull in the City Watch and pay the bribes needed to let the Hammer Guardians do as they will."

"And you still don't know where the food and supplies are going?"

Galessel shook her head. "We were hoping you might know or be able to find out."

The Dame worried a bit of lace between her fingers. "My, uh, resources. They are considerable, but this is not knowledge I have."

Galessel felt a bit of hope leave, like a grasshopper leaping from a leaf. It must have shown on her face, for the Dame's own softened and she said, "But again, I have considerable resources. I may be able to find something out."

A knock at the door startled them all. Galessel looked at the clock on the mantle. It was nearly midnight. This couldn't be a social call. They heard the Dame's butler head down the hall.

"Damn that sprite of a maid. Should have trusted my instincts and fired her ages ago. Quick, back out the way you came, but take a left at the third junction. It will get you closer to the inn, and the City Watch won't be waiting for you there. I'll be in touch."

Galessel grabbed her scarf and whispered a hasty "thank you" to the Dame before following Clove down the hall. Clove's covered hooves were quieter than Galessel's boots, and she hoped the Dame's rather loud protestations at being woken up at such an hour covered the sound. That woman was feisty, and Galessel found herself becoming quite fond of her.

Clove eased the cellar door shut and tiptoed down the stairs. "I did my best to move the boxes in front of the door, but that won't stop them if they're really looking." Her ear turned backward and her eyes widened. Clove grabbed Galessel's arm and urged her forward. "They got past the Dame. We better hurry."

Once again, Galessel found herself running through narrow passages to evade trouble. But these weren't magically silenced. The strike of her heels on the brick floor echoed around her, making it impossible to tell if they were being followed or not. Galessel followed close on Clove's heels, trusting her friend knew the way. The sunstone she held tight in her hand provided just enough light for Clove to see by. She trusted in her friend's ability to see well in the dark and prayed their small light wouldn't give their pursuers any aid.

They ran by a side tunnel, and then another and another. Galessel was sure she could hear the sounds of pursuit. Men's voices echoed around them. Clove stopped in front of her, and she nearly collided with the faun.

"We missed the turn, didn't we?"

Clove nodded, her eyes wide and her ears twitching. "Should have taken that last tunnel." She bounded back the way they'd come, and Galessel was hard-pressed to catch her.

Light blossomed in the tunnel just as Galessel turned into what she prayed was the right juncture. She caught up to Clove. "They're not far behind. I don't know if they saw me turn." Clove said nothing, but her ears swiveled to catch the sounds behind them, and she picked up the pace. Galessel, her breath coming in shorter and shorter gasps, did her best to keep up. It'd been a long time since she'd run with Clove. Even as children she'd never been able to keep up for long distances.

Just when Galessel thought her legs would turn to jelly and her lungs would burst, Clove slowed, and their little sunstone's light reflected off of a latch on a door in front of them.

"Please let it not be locked," Clove whispered.

It wasn't, but the hinges nigh screamed when they opened the door. "Asher must be having fun tonight," Clove swore. "Not even the god of luck could help us after that."

The door squealed just as loudly when they closed it. "Keep an eye out for the Watch. I'm going to find something to keep this door shut," Clove ordered.

Galessel looked around, thankful her eyes were used to the dark. They were in an alley, but not the one they'd entered the tunnels from. This one was clogged with debris—old crates, a lopsided cart missing a wheel and several planks from its bed, a shattered bed frame, and piles of stinking refuse. Galessel froze.

Hundreds of shining eyes reflected the light of the sunstone, making the alley appear to sparkle. She couldn't see who or what it was. Just shimmering eyes, all watching her. A shiver went down her spine, but she held her ground and stared back. "Any luck, Clove? We need to move, and quickly."

"Oof! Yeah, I know they're getting closer. I'm working on it. I could use your help."

Galessel could hear Clove pushing something heavy behind her. She glared at the eyes staring back at her and hoped it was intimidating enough to keep them away. She turned to help Clove push a large crate piled with trash in front of the door. "No, I didn't mean the Watch in the tunnels. There's something in this alley, and I'm praying it's not what I think it is."

Clove looked up at her, "What do you mean?"

Galessel didn't want to name her fear. If she was right, calling them out by name would cause them to attack. "Let's just say I hope it's just rats infesting this alley."

Clove gave the crate one last shove and slowly stood up straight. She'd caught on to what Galessel wasn't saying. "Right." The faun looked up and down the alley and pointed to the left. "Slow and steady then."

They tried to hurry without appearing to be alarmed, while they kept their eyes on the piles of trash and their inhabitants. Clove and Galessel were almost to the end of the alley when the sound of shattering wood disturbed the otherwise quiet night. The eyes in the refuse blinked as one and turned toward the sound.

"Move!" Galessel hissed. She and Clove ran, their tired limbs given new life by the startling sound of a thousand tiny battle cries headed toward the noise.

Galessel and Clove burst from the alley into the street. The sight of twin gargoyles just down the way was a welcome respite from the evening's travails. This late at night, the street was deserted. Too tired to worry about decorum, they jogged to the Copper Pony and breathlessly asked the stone guardians for leave to enter.

"You will always be welcome here, princess," the one on the left replied. "The wee brownie warriors will have their fill tonight and will sing your praises," the other remarked, nodding toward the alley.

"Peaceful slumber dear guests," the gargoyles said in unison.

Galessel and Clove each gave one a good scratch along their spinal ridge before slipping quietly into the inn.

Safely back in their room, Clove listened at the door before joining Galessel on the bed. "Galey, you're not going to like this, and I can't be sure, but I think I may have heard the butler announce Davorin's name."

Galessel's stomach turned sour. She cradled her face in her hands. "Oh Goddess, no."

"Maybe that's not a bad thing though, if you think about it," Clove said.

Galessel could hear her removing her hoof covers. The rubber devices plonked on the floor. Galessel thought about Clove's statement, following her own train of thought. "If I'm thinking what you're thinking, it might not be. If they'd caught us, he'd be lauded as a hero for rescuing the Dame from villainous fae, but since we weren't there, and his guards 'disappeared,' he can pawn off the visit as one of concern for her safety, and the Dame can't lodge a complaint against him."

"Exactly." Clove's eyes lit up with hope.

"But he's Svellvega. Would he care about appearances?"

Clove shrugged. "He sits at Victoria's right hand. He didn't get there by being a vulgar pirate captain. He needs her, and he wouldn't jeopardize that."

"Let's hope for the Dame's sake that you're right."

DAME BLANKENSHIP

CHAPTER 16

A note came several days later in a plain envelope with no insignia on the wax seal.

In remembrance of your recent loss, flowers and a fruit basket will be sent to 524 Rambart Lane, East Windsey, Arturia. A gentleman at the back entrance will have them for you promptly Sunday at 10 p.m.

Yours in grieving,

DB

"Not the most subtle or cryptic message, but simple enough to throw off the most base of snoopers," Clove commented after Galessel finished reading the note.

Galessel glanced at the day's *Ashelon Independent*, looking for the date. "That gives us two days to rally the fae and get to the bottom of this."

"Rally the fae? For what? You can't expect a bunch of merchants and artisans to storm whatever this address is on the word of a human noble."

"We tell them what we suspect: that the food sent by the Hidden Lands is there. That Victoria is keeping it from them and lying about it."

"And then what? We still don't know why. Bringing other fae into this will just get more of them killed. Or did you forget the hanging in the square?"

Clove's words stung. Galessel would never forget what happened, or the innocents who lost their lives because of her. She almost said as much, but the look on Clove's face stopped her. The faun's ears were laid flat against her head and her nostrils flared. Her friend was well and truly angry. "What have I said that's angered you so?"

Clove huffed and paced the room. "I love you, Galey, but you have no idea just how cruel humans can be. Even after all we've been through recently, you still want to run headlong into danger and drag a bunch of innocents with you." Clove stopped to face her. "It's time to ask your parents for help. Whatever is going on is bigger than some simple plot to deprive the fae and fuel hatred toward them. We need people who can take on the Hammer Guardians or whatever thugs may be guarding this shipment, because we can't do it ourselves. Chaun's been looking out for us, but you and I both know we can't rely on luck forever."

Galessel knew Clove was right, but the possibility of being forcibly returned to the Hidden Lands was too great. "We can't go back to the townhouse, Clove. You know the household will be on alert, and there will probably be Royal Guards there waiting. They'll scoop me up and send me back through the portal without a word."

Clove huffed again. "Galey, you are infuriatingly stubborn, you know that? Who says you have to go? I have as much pull with the townhouse staff and guards as you do, and they're not likely to toss me through the portal without an explanation."

"No, but they could still arrest you." It wasn't very likely. Clove enjoyed a measure of immunity due to her status as a messenger, but Galessel was feeling petulant.

She knew her friend was right, but it didn't make it any easier to agree to her plan. She already felt useless, and having to sit at the inn while Clove went to enlist aid didn't help. She glanced at Clove, who glared back with a look that brooked no argument. Galessel sighed and flopped onto the bed. "Fine. You're right. Dormond will at least listen to you before ordering the guards to arrest you."

"Dormond won't have me arrested. Just trust me in this, won't you?"

"Fine. But if you're not back in two hours, I'm coming after you."

Clove's ears perked up just a little bit. "Deal."

Galessel gripped her tea cup tighter as the hands on her pocket watch slowly moved toward four o'clock. Clove's two hours were nearly up. Galessel's stomach churned with anxiety. Unable to sit any longer, she stood and started gathering her belt pouch and cloak.

She was reaching for the door when it opened, nearly hitting her in the nose.

"Oh! Sorry Galey," Clove said as she took in Galessel's clothes. An ear twitched in the direction of the stairs as clock in the main hall chimed the hour. "I know I was pushing the time a bit close. Sorry about that."

Galessel backed up to let Clove in and saw a tall, dark-skinned human behind her. He didn't follow Clove inside but instead gave Galessel a deep bow. A few black dreadlocks escaped their tie and fell beside his face. As he straightened, he said, "Your Highness, please let me introduce myself. I am Navarre Vonai, former captain of the Queen's Guard and defender of the people." His accent was odd. Galessel heard mostly the smooth cadence of the Gallian coast, but there was something else that gave certain words a different lilt. She couldn't place it. She looked from him to Clove, unsure of what to think of this man standing before her in a suit of patchwork.

"He can be trusted, Galey. Let him in and close the door. I have a lot to tell you."

CHAPTER 17

"**I** couldn't get to the townhouse. There were uniformed Arturian guards and a few plain-clothed Watch around it," Clove explained. She sat next to Galessel on the bed, while Navarre took up the one chair, sitting with his arms crossed over the back, facing them.

Their room at the inn seemed much smaller with Navarre in it. He wasn't an overly large man, but his presence filled the room in a way Galessel had only experienced a few times before. His suit, though patchwork, was well made of fine, colorful fabrics. It fit him well and accentuated, rather than hid, his muscular frame. A well-made rapier hung at his hip. If he really had been captain of the Queen's Guard at some point in the past, then he knew how to use it.

"So now what do we do?" Galessel had to make herself focus on the matters at hand.

"I managed to get a message to Dormond, but I have no idea if he'll act on it, or will be able to with the townhouse surrounded by Arturian Guard." Clove looked to Navarre.

"Knowing what I know now, the story your people have been given is that the Guard is there for their protection, but everyone involved knows truly that it is to keep your people from interfering. I would expect there are more soldiers hidden away than even you saw, Clove. Her majest—Victoria will know everything that happens at the townhouse."

"No help from home. So now what?" Galessel rubbed a hand across her face. They needed the fae in Arturia. There was no getting around it.

"I know the area where the Dame is sending you. It is well-guarded, but a small force of skilled fighters could be successful."

"Are we to assume you know such a force?" Galessel didn't know if she should be hopeful or skeptical about Navarre's answer.

"I do," he said. And then he and Clove laid out their plan.

❀ ❀ ❀

The Drunken Boar wasn't a bad establishment, but it was no Rose and Rapier. Galessel's boots stuck to the floor and it smelled of stale beer and pipe smoke. But the tables were clean and the serving staff was courteous, even if the clientele was a bit rough. Galessel felt a little out of place in her upscale day dress and updo that hid her ears. Clove looked equally out of place in her overly large hat and blue dress. But there was nothing to be done about it. They were still wanted.

Galessel sipped her tea while they waited for Navarre to arrive. She missed her grandmother's coffee. Sniffing the steam coming from her teacup didn't have the same heady, energizing effect. Coffee in Arturia was expensive, and only the finer establishments even offered it any more. Because of its scarcity, it was now a drink of high society. If their two worlds went to war, she wondered how long it would be before the citizens of Arturia forgot the taste of coffee all together.

The pub's door opened, admitting a motley group of people. A male sylph in a brown leather vest and trousers chatted animatedly with a brownie on his shoulder. The sylph's wings shimmered purple, indicating he was both happy and excited. They were followed by two women, both obviously warriors, but judging from their clothes, they were from vastly different parts of the world. One wore menace like a glove. Clad in dark leather with a trefoil hat shadowing her face, she walked through the room as if she owned it. A rapier much like Navarre's hung from her hip along with a large pistol. The other woman was calm and bright in contrast in a bright red quilted jacket over a patterned skirt of a matching hue. Her dark hair was braided with tiny bells that tinkled with every step. If not for the twin curved daggers in her belt, one might mistake her for a holy person from the East. Navarre entered last, his colorful patchwork seeming to draw the group together. He was dressed more casually today in a pair of red and blue patchwork pants and a cream shirt with ties at the wrists, his rapier at his side. Today his dreadlocked hair was pulled back into a half ponytail, leaving some of it to fall free down his back. Galessel noted the way his hairstyle accented his cheekbones, and then immediately chastised herself for such thoughts. This was not the time or place.

Navarre spied them and led the group over to their corner table. He waved amicably at the waitress, who left the table she was serving with a bit too much haste to follow. After the group ordered drinks, Navarre introduced his friends.

"Mademoiselle Clove, Mademoiselle Galessel," he said. "This is my former second in command, Morgan O'Shea."

The woman in the trefoil hat nodded. "It is good to see you again, Clove, and a pleasure to meet you, Galessel."

The others were introduced as Samga, a skilled archer from the steppes of Shenzhou; Eirsal the sylph; and Widget, a brownie of Clan Difyr.

They waited until the waitress had left, at some urging by Widget to "find somewhere else to fawn," before discussing the plan Navarre and Clove had laid out the night before.

The plan was to wait for the wagonload of food and supplies to be brought in, follow it to its final destination, and hopefully find out why Victoria was hoarding it.

As talk swirled around her about how to accomplish their mission, Galessel was shocked at the casual way they talked about killing the guards and sentries that would inevitably get in their way. Even Clove didn't seem to have a problem with it.

"A moment please," Galessel interrupted Navarre's reply to where Morgan might best hide with her long rifle to snipe guards from a longer range. "Is there no way to incapacitate the sentries without resorting to murder?"

Eirsal, his wings an odd shade of puce Galessel had never seen, replied in a whisper, "It's well known to those in the area that the Hammer Guardians control that neighborhood. They would kill you and me in a heartbeat. Why should we not do the same?"

"Galessel, you are not a soldier, but the rest of us are, in our own ways. I am sorry such talk disturbs you, but there is no other way if we want to survive this encounter," Navarre stated with a hint of sadness in his voice.

Hammer Guardians were subject to summary execution under the Multi-Realm Treaty of 1811, but

Galessel still didn't like the idea of being the executioner. She closed her eyes for a moment, thinking she might be able to use the remains of her grandmother's sleep powder or her silver tongue, but too many things could go wrong. She opened her eyes again. "Very well. My apologies for interrupting. You were saying?"

Navarre went on to describe in detail the warehouse and surrounding buildings. Galessel listened while the others planned, and wondered if she would be useful at all.

CHAPTER 18

The plan, in theory, was simple. Navarre would disable the wagon guard and take his place—how, Galessel wasn't sure, but Navarre assured her it would be easy. Then as the wagon passed by them, Morgan would distract the driver and Galessel and Clove would hop on the back, hiding under the tarp. Simple.

But the way things had gone for her and Clove lately, Galessel was sure something would go wrong. She sent a quick prayer to Donnan and brushed opposite hands over her shoulders in a gesture meant to wipe away errant webs of fate. Clove twitched an ear at the sound but didn't turn from watching the street. They waited in the shadows of an alley for Navarre to pass by in the wagon. Morgan and her lover were across the street, chatting in front a pub. Morgan's long red hair stood out in stark contrast to her black leather outfit. Her lady was much more demure in a brown walking dress that highlighted the olive tone of her skin. They were quite the picture of contrasts.

Butterflies started to churn the acid in Galessel's stomach. "Clove, they're late."

Clove checked her pocket watch, a bright flash of silver in her otherwise black ensemble. "Not yet. Still a few minutes to go." Her ears swiveled. "Never mind, they're here. Get ready."

Morgan and her friend didn't seem to notice the carriage. In fact, just as it was rounding the corner, Morgan embraced the woman and kissed her passionately, breaking apart only a moment before the wagon reached them. With a swagger, Morgan stepped into the street, flourishing her trefoil hat. "Until tomorrow, darling!" She blew a kiss to her lover as she continued to walk backward, seemingly oblivious to the oncoming wagon.

The wagon driver hauled back on the reins, cursing at Morgan. The horses stopped just inches from the leather-clad woman. "Oy! Watch it." Morgan yelled at the driver, holding up her hand in what Galessel assumed was an obscene gesture. Both Navarre and the driver yelled at Morgan, who only became more belligerent.

"Come on, Galey. It's now or never." Clove grabbed her hand and pulled her out of the alley. They ran to the back of the wagon and crawled under the tarp. They'd barely gotten settled when the wagon started rolling. They wedged themselves between two rows of crates and as far from the back of the wagon as they could get. It wasn't comfortable, but they wouldn't be there for long. It was pitch black under the tarp, making the ride disorienting and claustrophobic.

They hadn't been under tarp for more than a few minutes when she heard Clove gag.

"Are you okay, Clove?" Galessel whispered.

"Chaun has either forsaken us or is having a laugh right now, damn him," Clove replied. "I smell pickled salamander eggs."

Galessel felt her own gorge rise at the thought. She was thankful her nose wasn't as sharp as Clove's. "I think this is more the work of Asher, than the god of luck. If being forced to ride with salamander eggs once again isn't the definition of strife, I don't know what is."

"We better get there soon, or I'm going to lose my dinner."

Galessel agreed, and reached out a hand to Clove in commiseration. She hoped this would be the worst of it.

❁ ❁ ❁

The wagon stopped. Galessel could hear a muffled exchange, the creaking of wooden doors opening, and then the wagon started to move again. They hadn't moved far when she heard the distinct *thwap-thwap* of a pair of arrows hitting their mark, followed soon after by the thud of bodies hitting the ground.

Galessel hated that men would die today. But there was a part of her that felt that justice was being served. These were Hammer Guardians—members of the same group that had murdered innocent fae in order to send a message and flush her and Clove out. If what they did today saved other innocent lives, then she would find a way to come to terms with it.

The wagon wobbled for a moment, and then light blossomed as Navarre threw back the tarp. Galessel blinked against the warehouse's bright lights. She didn't see the driver. He was probably dead. *"Allez-vous!"* Navarre urged before turning his back to them and jumping off the wagon.

Clove leapt from the wagon, using the horses for cover from anyone to their left. Once her eyes adjusted, Galessel stood and looked for a target. Crates, bales of wool, and bags of flour arranged in orderly rows filled the space in front of the horses. Catwalks on either side of the warehouse were empty, but each was connected to a set of stairs that led up to the second story. The only target she could see was a guard just inside the door, and he was taking aim at Navarre. She aimed her rifle and began to squeeze the trigger. She knew the basics of using a firearm, but her aim wasn't precise, which is why Navarre had given her one that shot nets instead of bullets. All she had to do was aim at the heads of the people in front of her and shoot. The net would do the rest. She hoped. There hadn't been time to practice with the weapon.

A loud retort behind her spooked her and the horses. She jerked, and her shot went wide. The net fell harmlessly over a stack of crates. At the same time the horses lurched forward. Galessel was so intent on watching her target that she didn't see the top of the warehouse door. It clipped her forehead, sending her tumbling backward off the wagon.

Dazed, Galessel stared at the sky for a moment as she tried to puzzle out what had happened. Her head throbbed, but she didn't feel any blood. The sound of a pistol shot, followed by the hiss and splat of a steam ball brought Galessel's attention to the square just in time to see Eirsal sink below the edge of the roof across from her, screaming. The sound was so high-pitched; it was like a pin through her ear. She'd never heard a sylph scream like that. It couldn't be good. Dogs all through the neighborhood started barking. She heard a couple more arrows whiz by and the thud of another body hitting the courtyard's stones.

Morgan came running to her while yelling over her shoulder, "Samga, get to Eirsal!" She held out a hand to Galessel and helped her up. "Are you all right?"

Galessel nodded and immediately regretted the action. Her head throbbed even more. "Ouch. Yes. What just happened?"

Morgan pulled her to the side of the doors and peeked inside the warehouse. "We've taken out all the guards out here, but Eirsal got hit with a steam-ball. I don't know how bad he's hurt." She took another peek. "Come on. We need to help the others." Morgan ran inside, crouching low. Galessel followed suit.

As they came around the door, Galessel saw Clove, still near the head of the wagon, shoot a guard with her steam-powered rifle. Her shot hit him in the shoulder but didn't seem to affect him. The guard rushed at her, a heavy club raised above his head. Transfixed, Galessel watched as Clove did nothing, letting the man get closer. Galessel knew Clove had a pistol as well, and only belatedly realized what the faun was up to. The guard closed on Clove and was bringing his club down to hit her, when Clove finally reacted. She leapt into the air and kicked the man with both feet, directly in the chest. The impact threw him into a stack of flour sacks. At least one exploded, creating a fog of white powder.

A bullet whizzed past Galessel's ear. She heard it splat on the wooden floor behind her.

"Down!" Morgan yelled at her. At the same time, Galessel felt a weight hit her from the side, pushing her to the ground. "Stay down," Morgan said in her ear. The smell of flour, gunpowder, and Morgan's musky cologne filled Galessel's nose. Gunshots echoed from all directions in the warehouse.

Galessel froze. The world seemed to tip on its side. The edges of her vision went wavy and it was hard to breathe. With Morgan's weight on her back, and the smell of gunpowder and the occasional scream from man or horse, she wasn't sure where she was anymore. She fought the urge to scream. She squirmed under Morgan's weight, desperate to get away.

"Easy, girl," Morgan whispered. "When I move, roll to your right and get up against those crates and stay there until I say so." And then her weight was gone. Galessel rolled until she hit something solid. A steamball hit where she'd just been. She curled up and tried to catch her breath. She wasn't on the *Intrepid*. She was in Arturia, fighting the Hammer Guardians. She was with friends. Clove! She looked for her friend but couldn't find her the cloud of flour. Across from her two guards on the catwalk were looking for targets. She still had the net rifle clutched to her chest. She couldn't just sit there.

Galessel looked to her left, where Morgan had gone. The fiery-haired woman was standing just under the edge of the catwalk closest to them, firing both pistols into the wooden planks as fast as she could. The catwalk shook as the man above Morgan fell. Blood began to leak through the ruined planking. Morgan glanced over at her. "Behind you!"

Galessel stood up, aimed at the guard looking down on her, and fired. The net hit him in the face and chest, pushing him backward. He screamed as he fell over the far side. The net caught on something, saving him from hitting the ground, but the momentum of the fall caused the net to swing violently into the wall. The guard within lay limp. She cocked the rifle again and turned around in time to see Clove jump straight up, aiming her pistol at one of the guards on the catwalk across from her. Just at the top of her arc, she turned and fired at the second guard, missing. Galessel looked at the first guard, curious as to why Clove changed her target, and then regretted it. Widget attacked Clove's initial target, the brownie's long claws ripping flesh from bone. The guard didn't have time to scream before Widget had torn out his throat. The brownie leapt from the shredded body and ran at the second guard.

The man screamed, "Asher's balls! What are you?" and started firing his pistols at the brownie. Widget was fast, but not faster than a hail of bullets. Galessel watched in horror as the brownie's small body was suddenly flung backward off the catwalk. He landed hard on a bale of wool and did not move.

She started to run to Widget but was thrown to the ground, this time by the heat and force of an explosion. Flaming bits of wood and debris rained down around her. She covered her head and waited for her ears to quit ringing. Morgan's touch on her shoulder nearly stopped her heart.

"It's over. At least for now," the woman told her. Morgan offered her a hand up, again.

"Is everyone okay?" Galessel asked, knowing the answer for at least one of them was no. "And what was that explosion?"

Morgan shook her head. The musketeer looked nonplussed by what they'd just been through. "You can thank Samga and her exploding arrows for ending this. Although the whole neighborhood will be up now. As for the rest, I don't know where Navarre is and I can't speak for anyone else. I'm going to get up on that catwalk and see what I can see. It looks like the horses are standing on some kind of trap door or ramp. There were too many guards here for a space this small. There's got to be more to this warehouse." And with that, Morgan turned and made her way up to the catwalk using the stacks of crates for stairs.

Unsure of what else to do, Galessel made her way over to where Widget had fallen. She nearly slipped in the flour in her haste, catching herself against one of the draft horses. It snorted at her and stomped a hoof the size of a dinner plate. She patted it on the neck and kept going, careful to stay clear of the flour and the horses.

She found Clove hunched over a bale of wool, her hands doing something with a twist of batting. Her ears were droopy and Galessel thought she heard her friend crying. Galessel approached and put a gentle hand on Clove's shoulder. "Is he all right?"

Clove sniffed. "No. Gentle Goddess, no." She began to sob and turned to Galessel. "He's gone."

Clove's words didn't register right away. She pulled her friend into a hug. It was only when Galessel peeked over Clove's shoulder at Widget's lifeless form did it hit her. One arm was missing—everything below the shoulder was gone. Clove had tried to bandage the wound, but it had been too late. The wool bale he'd landed on was soaked with blood. The little brownie was too small to survive such a grievous injury. Tears stung her eyes, and she hugged Clove close. "He was a fierce warrior. He will be welcomed into Freyka's halls as a hero, and Clan Difyr will sing songs about him for generations." Clove sobbed even harder, and Galessel let her own tears fall. None of them were supposed to get hurt.

"Galessel, you should come see this," Morgan's alto voice echoed in the now quiet confines of the warehouse.

Galessel didn't move until Clove pushed back from her, wiping her nose on her sleeve. "Go. I'll be fine." She pulled a handkerchief from her pocket and covered Wicket's still form. "I'll go look for Navarre. You see what Morgan's found."

Galessel wiped the tears from her eyes and walked to where she could see Morgan standing at the near end of the catwalk. "There's a trap door in this corner." She pointed with her pistol toward the corner where the warehouse met the back wall of the shop. "Head down that row of crates there and take a right. You can't miss it." Galessel nodded. She hurried by the guard Clove had kicked. His chest was caved in, his gray shirt dark with blood. His eyes were wide open, the shock of the kick frozen on his face.

The row of crates Morgan had led her to was stacked nearly ten feet high on both sides. Some were stamped with the names of companies and seemed to belong to Kinsey's General Goods, the store in front of the warehouse. There were crates of colorful fabrics from Aryadi, a few bales of raw cotton from Zhupatra, and dozens of other general items the people of Arturia needed. But nothing of what she saw looked like goods from the Hidden Lands. Would she find what she was looking for wherever the trap door led? Galessel reached the end of the row and turned right, lost in her thoughts. A few steps later, she stopped dead in her tracks.

It was the gold hoop in his ear that set Galessel's heart racing. She didn't have to see the pointed ears he hid under his wool cap, or the glacier blue eyes beneath dark brows to know what he was. She saw the same curve of the gold earring every night in her nightmares. Svellvega. She started walking backward, slowly. She didn't have her gun—she'd left it by the catwalk—but it was empty anyway. Her hands went to her sides and pulled the thin knives from her corset. She took another step back and was stopped by a wall of muscle. A thick arm wrapped around her before she could run, pinning her arms to her sides, while a meaty hand clamped over her mouth, muffling her cry for help.

"Well, what have we got here?" The man holding her said. His raspy voice sent chills running from her scalp to her toes. She locked her knees to keep them from buckling. The combined smell of stale sweat and whale oil that engulfed her captor made her gag.

The Svellvega in front of her walked closer, twirling his pistol around his finger. He stopped just shy of losing the safely behind the row of crates, out of sight of Morgan's deadly aim. "Turn her head, Zegrath, I want to see her ears. She's got the look of an elf."

Fingers dug into her cheek, pulling her face to one side. She fought, but her captor had better leverage. She felt heat rise in her face, and her ears began to throb. She cried out against the hand over her mouth. They'd already cut off her ear tips. What would they do to her now?

"*Sikevra*! I heard about you. Captain Murik likes to brag about what he did to you. I wonder, will your parents still pay a ransom for you, Anisbarii whore?" He aimed the gun at her head. "But then again, the price on your head's not bad either, and we don't have to keep you alive for that."

Her captor chuckled, and he pulled her in closer, his arm like a steel band across her chest. The world slowed down and the sounds around her slipped away. In a strange moment of calm, everything seemed to change. She'd been a Svellvega captive once. She wouldn't be put through that again. She'd get free or die trying. The world came rushing back: the sound of wind chimes, the smell of rancid whale oil, burnt wool and flesh, the breeze from the open warehouse door. She pulled up her foot, and in her best imitation of Clove, stomped down with all her might on the foot of her captor. She felt something break under her heel, and he cursed. His arm was suddenly gone from her torso, and she could breathe. She dove into the aisle at the same time the other Svellvega fired at her. She hit the floor hard and rolled, clambering to get back up and face her enemy. The Svellvega who'd held her fell forward across the aisle. Blood pooled beneath his chest.

"*Madla Mai*! You're dead now." The first Svellvega rounded the corner, his gun aimed low. As he raised it, a shot rang out from behind her. He rocked backward, blood blossoming across his chest. With a determined look, he stepped forward and raised his gun again. Three more shots rang out. His body jerked with each impact before he fell to his knees and slumped to the ground.

Galessel stood there, her heart hammering in her chest. A hand touched her shoulder. She spun, the knife in her hand glanced off of the lacquered blue and silver armor of her family's Royal Guard. "Oh!"

The guard before her took off his helmet and knelt, his head bowed. "Forgive me, Princess. I did not mean to scare you." He raised his head. It was Erindor, her personal guard. "Are you well?"

She'd never been so happy to see him. His hair was slicked against his head with sweat and his face was flushed. The Guards must have run all the way from the family townhouse. She took a deep breath and considered his words. All things considered, she was. "I'm fine, Erindor, and grateful for your intervention." She looked behind him to two other guards. "And to you as well." They bowed. She returned her attention to Erindor, who'd returned to standing and was checking the charge on his hydronium gun. "I don't know if there are more Svellvega. We thought the warehouse was clear before."

Just then, Navarre and Clove came around the far end of the row. Navarre was wiping his sword off on a scrap of fabric. "I think I got the last one." His shirt was torn, and he was limping. A makeshift bandage cinched his thigh. "But it wouldn't hurt to do another sweep." Navarre looked over Galessel's shoulder at the dead Svellvega. "Those men are not Hammer Guardians or City Watch. Who are they?"

"Svellvega," Galessel spat. "Enemies of the Hidden Lands, and apparently allies of Victoria's."

Navarre squatted by one of the bodies and started going through the pockets. He found nothing but a few coins, which he pocketed. He took the hat off and looked inside the rim. He pulled a small swatch of fabric from it. His eyes seemed to linger on the body's ears for a moment before he stood and brought the fabric to Galessel. It was black, with the head of a snarling snow bear stamped on it in red dye.

"It's the Svellvega emblem, but why have it inside a hat? Is it a token of some sort?" Galessel asked of no one in particular.

"Your Highness, if I may?" A Royal Guard, with a golden star in his ear indicating a captain's rank, held out his hand for the bit of fabric. Galessel nodded and handed it over. "Tokens like this are easily passed from hand to hand and are meant as an easy way to show allegiance for those who are attempting to hide within enemy ranks. We've captured a few since the Great Unveiling, and if I'm not mistaken, these particular tokens mark these elves as members of the Bear Fang clan—a particularly violent and ruthless sect within the Svellvega. You are lucky to have survived this encounter, Princess."

Galessel nodded to Erindor and the others. "I would not have if it hadn't been for you."

"If I may interrupt," Navarre began. "The sounds of battle will draw the City Watch, even to this neighborhood. We should leave soon."

Galessel motioned to the other Royal Guards. "You two, check the warehouse again. The rest of you, come with me. I was on my way to investigate a trap door when I was stopped by the Svellvega."

"As you wish," Navarre and Erindor said in unison. Clove stifled a giggle. The men looked at each other.

Navarre shrugged and motioned for Galessel to lead the way.

❀ ❀ ❀

The trap door led to a basement that appeared to be as wide as the warehouse above but stretched far into the darkness beyond their lanterns. There was an open space beneath what they had assumed was a ramp from above. A large wheel attached to chains that went up through the floor was situated to one side. The rest of the enormous space was filled with crates of supplies, food, and hydronium.

The three of them explored for several minutes before rejoining. "It's mostly Hidden Lands goods, Highness," Erindor noted. "Ever-fresh runes on enough food for every fae in Arturia and beyond. And I found ammunition for weapons and cannon."

"*Mon deu.* They are preparing for war," Navarre said, his voice barely a whisper.

They all stood in silence. Galessel knew war with Ashelon was a possibility, but this made it real. Could the Hidden Lands survive a war with Ashelon with the Svellvega as their allies?

Clove broke the silence by clearing her throat. "I found several doors, locked with goblin locks, farther into the warehouse. They likely lead to a tunnel system similar to the one in Dame Blankenship's neighborhood."

"Good, we should find out where they lead," Navarre said.

Three short yips from above made them all start. Navarre looked up through the trap door, then back at Galessel. "You must go now, Princess. The City Watch is here. I will deal with it and the Hammer Guardians. Warn your people. We will meet soon." Navarre bowed to her and kissed her hand. "*Á la prochaine.*" Galessel's lack of comprehension must have registered on her face. Navarre smiled, his eyes crinkling with understanding. "Until we meet again, mademoiselle."

Galessel watched Navarre climb up the ladder and disappear through the trap door and was about to follow when Clove tugged on her sleeve.

"Galey, this way." Clove turned her in the opposite direction. "It's time to go home."

Galessel nodded and followed her companions into the darkness.

CHAPTER 19

A letter came by courier the next day. It was from Navarre. Galessel read it out loud to Clove while they sipped coffee in the drawing room of her family townhouse.

"I have good news, and bad, I'm afraid," he began.

Galessel groaned inwardly. Of course there was bad news. Lately it was all bad news.

"Might as well start with the bad," Clove said.

Galessel scanned the next passage. "He did." She continued reading aloud.

"The City Watch arrested the surviving Hammer Guardians, but they were released this morning on a technicality."

Galessel shouldn't have been surprised, but she was. "A technicality? What technicality?" She continued reading.

"Morgan informed me the magistrate claimed there was no evidence they were Hammer Guardians, and said the word of the shop owner that they were his hirelings was enough to release them without charges."

Clove nearly spit out her coffee. "What? Let me guess, the pins on their lapels were *lost* and the City Watchmen conveniently forgot the Hammer Guardians controlled that neighborhood in the first place."

Galessel read on silently, then nodded. "In addition, the price on our heads has now doubled. They kept the deaths of the Svellvega quiet, but word must have gotten back that fae were involved in the break-in last night."

"I'm not surprised. Did he mention Eirsal's condition?" The faun's ears drooped in anticipation of the answer.

Galessel scanned the letter and her heart suddenly felt like lead. "He did. They're hopeful he'll recover, but there was more in that steam-ball than just superheated water. They got him to the apothecary shop as quickly as they could, but the healer wasn't able to do much but ease his pain. She told them it appears that Eirsal was hit with cold iron."

Clove gasped and her eyes went wide. "Goddess, no. Cold iron? How did they get a hold of any?"

"I don't know. Chaun be praised none of the rest of us were hit with it." She choked back a mix of horror and anger. Cold iron, the rare metal found in falling stars, was something all fae feared. It was deadly to them. "One of Eirsal's wings was almost completely melted away, and his face was badly burned. He'll never fly again."

"It's a miracle he survived at all. The amount of cold iron must have been incredibly small." Clove sat quietly for a moment, thinking. Her serious face clashed with the cheerful color of her pink blouse. "You said he got hit with a steam-ball. We need to find out how they're incorporating the cold iron into them. If Victoria's army is armed with those, it would be devastating to our forces."

Galessel nodded, having come to the same conclusion herself. "I'll ask Navarre to see what he can find out. If the Goddess is kind, that ammunition is as rare as the element itself."

"So what's the good news?" Clove asked, motioning to the letter hanging from Galessel's hand.

Galessel wasn't sure she wanted to read anymore, even if it was good news. She didn't know if there was anything he could say to counter the distress his news had caused. But she read on. "He says, 'I spoke to a friend of mine, who is a reporter for the *Ashelon Independent*. I told him what we found, and he promised to do his own investigation. And, word has gotten out about the tunnel entrance to some of the trickier members of the fae community. There is a guard on the door now, but not before some of the goods went missing. I would not be surprised if they have a hard time keeping guards there, especially at night.'"

"So what do we do now?" Galessel wanted to use her gift to compel the fae and humans alike to riot in the street, demanding Victoria release the stores of supplies, but she knew that would only result in needless death, and likely a hardening of Victoria's resolve to keep them for her armies.

"We go home, Galey," Clove said with regret in her voice. "With the price on our heads, we can do nothing here, and we'd be a danger to anyone who harbors us. Tell your parents to stop sending shipments. They are not getting to your people and are only helping Victoria. Morgan, Navarre, and the others will do what they can to expose the Hammer Guardians."

Galessel felt less than useless. Was everything they'd done and the people they'd lost been in vain? She was forced to concede that Clove was right about going home. Truth be told, she missed the Hidden Lands, but she felt like she was giving up.

Her thoughts must have been plain on her face. Clove put a hand on hers and said, "We're not giving up, Galey. There is much we can do from home. This isn't over."

Her ears throbbed suddenly, but she resisted touching them. The Svellvega were players on this game board, too. Maybe it was time to focus her attention there, take them off the board, while Navarre worked to weaken the queen here.

Flush with new purpose, she couldn't wait to go home.

✾ ✾ ✾

Galessel sat at a small table under the trees in her family's garden, sipping a cup of her grandmother's coffee. A copy of the *Ashelon Independent* lay on the table. The headline read, "Hammer Guardians Exposed in Arturia."

Galessel sniffed the steam from her cup and smiled.

To Be Concluded in *Fallana Sian*.

Glossary

Dien-Vek   An elven banishment ritual involving the removal of the tips of an elf's ears.

Fallana Sian   An elven forgiveness ceremony often held to reverse the banishment from *Dien-Vek*.

Madla-mai   A strong elven curse, similar in meaning to 'son-of-a-bitch'.

Nodgoddim   The common tongue of the Hidden Lands

Ravela   A bird-like humanoid creature with brightly colored feathers. Flocks of ravela often play off the bows of fae airships.

R'vikki   An intelligent cat-like race.

Sikevra   An outcast. An elf subjected to the *Dien-Vek* becomes *sikevra*.

ABOUT THE AUTHOR

Carolyn Kay is a scientist by day, and an author, dancer, knitter, and herbalist by night. She's attempting to raise two fine felines with the help of her husband, Chaz Kemp. (The results are mixed. *Looking at you, Sif*) She also occasionally channels a fae changeling, named Cinder. You can catch up on her latest shenanigans at carolynkayauthor.com, or on Twitter @bewitchinghips.

ABOUT THE ARTIST

Chaz Kemp is the self-described Art Monkey Supreme behind all of the fabulous art of Ashelon. His origins are clouded in fantastical mystery. Was he found under a rock as his mother claims, or is he really a fae son of the King of the Faeries? We may never know. What we do know is that Chaz is an accomplished artist, musician, actor, and fur-kid father. You can find him at ChazKemp. com and support his work at Patreon.com\chazkemp.

www.ingramcontent.com/pod-product-compliance
Lightning Source LLC
Chambersburg PA
CBHW020613120726
47905CB00003B/778